James Greig Badenoch

Art of Letter Painting Made Easy

James Greig Badenoch

Art of Letter Painting Made Easy

ISBN/EAN: 9783337390945

Printed in Europe, USA, Canada, Australia, Japan

Cover: Foto ©Andreas Hilbeck / pixelio.de

More available books at **www.hansebooks.com**

BY

JAMES GREIG BADENOCH

FOURTH EDITION

LONDON

CROSBY LOCKWOOD AND SON

7, STATIONERS' HALL COURT, LUDGATE HILL

1888

CONTENTS.

LETTER PAINTING MADE EASY.

Introductory.

HAVING followed the business of letter painting, or sign writing, for many years, and having worked on a system which I believe to be entirely my own—or at any rate I have never known or heard of any one using it, or, in fact, any system except the "rule of thumb;" and it must be admitted that some men can, and do, turn out some most beautiful specimens of letter painting without any gauge or guide beyond the trained eye—I have been induced to make my system public.

However creditable the work just referred to may be to those who have done it, it is but poor encouragement to the beginner, for he has a long and difficult task before him, and forty-nine out of every fifty give it up in despair, for he has no guide but his eye. In the hope of being of some assistance to the beginner, and, it may be, a help to many men, good at other branches of the trade of house painting, I have made public the system on which I work; having no doubt but that, to any one willing to try, it will prove a safe and sure guide.

And I may as well say here that it is not intended that the system is to be always used. It is only meant that the student should learn by this how to make and form a well-shaped letter, to know and have some sure plan how to get spaces and distances, and to ascertain when his work is correctly done. Here he can learn a system which is mathematically correct and beyond all dispute;

having acquired which, and being able to do without drawing so many lines—and this will very soon be the case—he may then break through all rules and suit his own fancy. When once he has mastered this, he has mastered all, so far as letter making goes. Then, with the help of colours and good taste, there is nothing in sign painting he may not do. As regards gilding and colouring, I will say nothing; the first is, as far as the laying on goes, a mere mechanical art, and the other can only be effective when produced by taste and judgment.

To Draw Plain Block Letters.

PLATE I. First, " snap " the line *a* on your black board, or draw it with a pencil on paper if more convenient; paper will be best for a while.   Then draw the line *b*.   Now whatever distance you may have between *a* and *b*, give twice that betwixt *b* and *c ;* then *c* and *d* will be the same distance apart as *a* and *b*.   Now you have got the length and thickness of your letter.   Next divide the length of your line with your compasses by the same space as you have between *a* and *b ;* having done that, roughly fill in the words " First Time," as you see it in the place at *a*, *b*, *c*, and *d*.

This being done, take a look at your work, and you will observe that F, R, S, T, all take up four spaces each ; that is, three for the letter and one for a space between the letters.   The two I's you will see take only two each ; that is, one for the

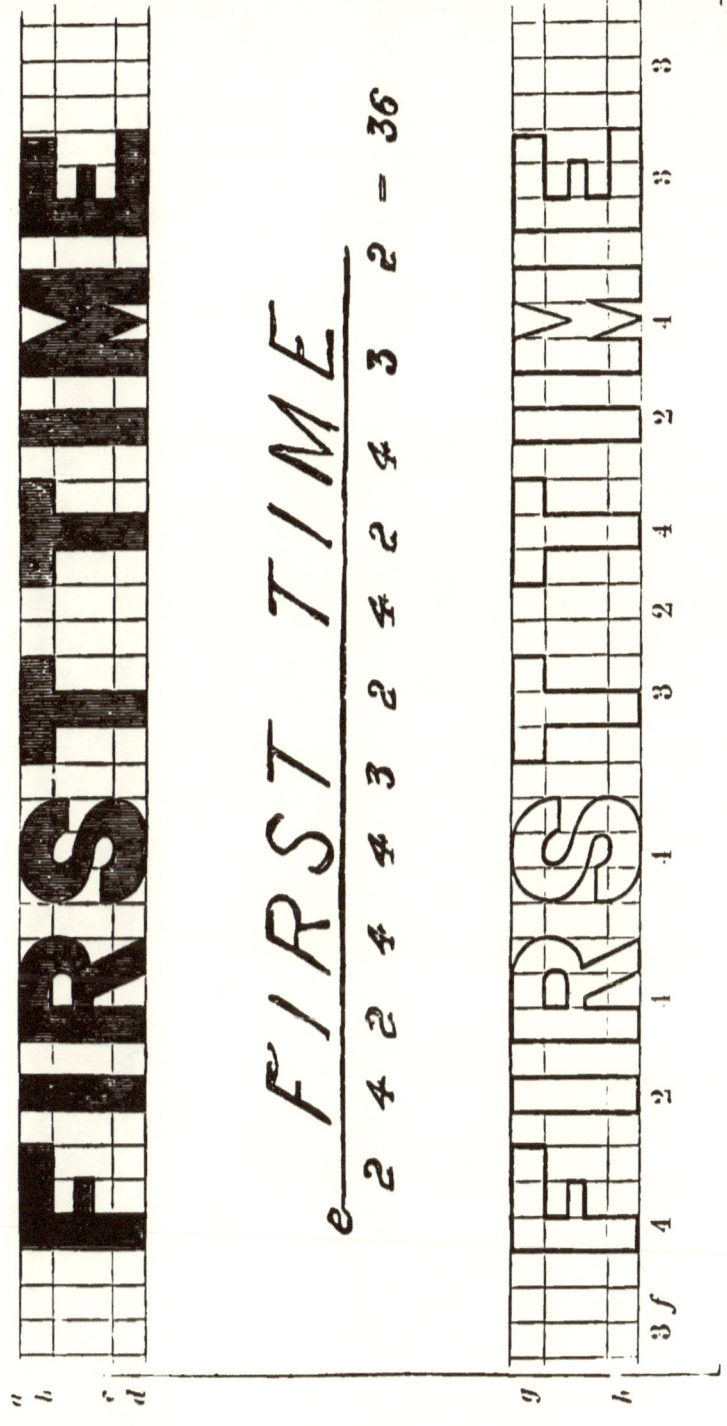

FIRST TIME

$$e \quad 2 \quad 4 \quad 4 \quad 2 \quad 3 \quad 4 \quad 4 \quad 3 \quad 2 \quad = 36$$

letter itself and one for the division between the letters.

Second (*e* on Plate I.), roughly sketch the words "First Time" as you see it here. Two are for the space left at the beginning of your board, or show-card; 4 for F with its space; 2 for I with its space, and so on, until you come to the two T's, when you must allow two for the space between them. Then go on in the same way for the word TIME, and allow two spaces after, in all thirty-six spaces.

Third, draw *f* (Plate I.); first divide the length of your paper, or whatever space you are going to allow for your letters, into thirty-six divisions. Do it either with your compasses, or take your rule, and having found your length in inches, divide it by thirty-six, and if you find that you have fractional parts over give them to the spaces at the ends. Having found the space you can allow, mark off from the top of your sign the distance at both ends, draw your line, then below that mark off and again draw your line, when you will have *g*; then mark off two spaces, draw a line at that, then another off and draw, when you will have *h*; now draw your perpendiculars.

Now miss two spaces and fill up the next three with the letter F, then miss one and fill in the letter I, and so on until you have written "First Time."

Having done all this, look at your work. What do you think of it? Are the letters what you would wish as to proportion—are they too thick or too thin, or what? The rule for making them is not a hard and fast one, but it is a rule that gives a very fair, proportionate letter; and when you have mastered the theory you can suit your own fancy. In the meantime you will be none the worse for sticking to this.

Before going any farther, take a look at the R, and see where it begins to curve; you will observe that every point of beginning and ending is indicated by the square, either for the curve or straight line, length, or thickness.

Now look at the letter S, that bugbear of all beginners, as well as of a good many that think something of themselves; mark how it is done; did you ever see anything more simple? Why, when you drew your straight lines it was formed; and so were all the letters, as you will soon find out, if you have not done so already. Well, how do you like your work thus far? No doubt it is rather rough, but we will mend that by-and-by.

Sign Painting

We will now suppose that the pupil has gone through the first steps with me, and that he sees his way clear so far. We will now begin to paint, say what—his own sign. I have not the pleasure of knowing his name, so I will call him Robert Burns, Painter. So Robert must measure the length of his sign-board, or if he has not got one, he must just imagine one the size he would like it to be when he turns " gaffer ; " and he has my best wishes towards his success when he begins. In the meantime we will go at

ROBERT BURNS, PAINTER.

Robert, having got the size of his sign, will measure the length of it; and as " Robert Burns " is composed of letters of four spaces each, and as there are eleven letters, he will just have four times eleven, with two spaces to be left at the

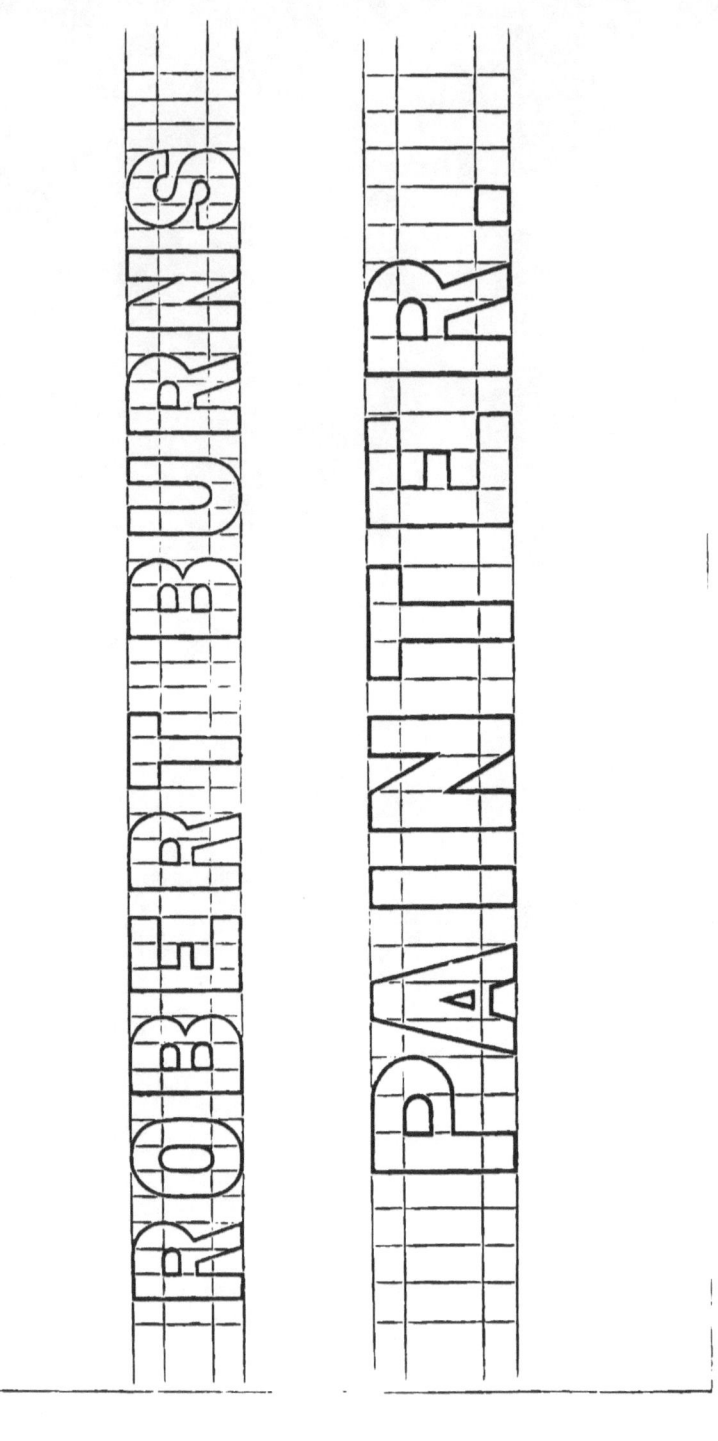

ROBERT BURNS

PAINTER.

beginning, three in the middle, or between the two words, and three at the end; that will be four times eleven $= 44 + 2 + 3 + 3 = 52$ in all, the number of spaces into which his sign is divided. But as I have allowed four spaces for each letter, and as no letter follows the S, there can be no space between, so the last letter can only take three spaces, therefore there will be only fifty-one spaces. Begin operations as follows :—

PLATE II. Having divided the length of the sign by fifty-one, mark that space from the top of it—this is generally a safe rule to go by—snap your line, giving the same space for the thickness of the top of your letter; then mark off twice that for the body of the letter; now once again for the lower part, and you have the full length of your letter. Having done so, draw your perpendiculars with the help of a square—either a T or an ordinary square will do, or you may make one of card-board, and by doubling up the edge you can slip it along by your top or bottom moulding; that being done, begin by filling up your spaces with the letters, first doing the third space with what would form the letter I; now draw a curved line beginning with a straight from the near top corner of what is now your I, carrying it straight until you come to the top of the second space of your letter, then curve until you get the corner formed by the junction of your fourth perpendicular with your second horizontal lines. But you cannot do better than look at the plate; it is plain enough.

Having chalked in all your letters in the top line, begin on your second the word PAINTER. Here you can run your word into the whole length of the space, or you can leave spaces at each end so as to be more in the centre, as in the plate, where you have thirty-five divisions. Leave five spaces and commence chalking out, taking particular notice where your curves begin and end.

PLATE III.

You will find that every point is indicated by the squares for curves, length, breadth, thickness, or angles, and by very little practice you will find them all with the greatest ease.

· To Draw Full Block Letters.

I will now try and show you how. to construct full block letters. They are made in the same way as those you have already done, only one space more must be allowed between each letter, which space is equally divided betwixt the letters, to form what is called the block.

PLATE III. Here you have what may be called two kinds of letters. The first line is composed of what may be termed plain blocks, and is about the boldest and easiest to read that there is; and in fact there is no more effective letter that can be painted for reading at a great distance. You will observe the T, it takes three spaces; but many like it better when it takes five, that is, one each for the drooping ends, and one between what may be called the pedestal and the drooping ends. Either way would be right; five looks best where you are not tied for room.

The second line is almost the same, the only difference being that the blocks are square as in the first line. They are slightly curved at the angles—a very pretty yet bold letter if carefully done. I do not see that they need much description, as the plate explains itself clearly enough; further on you will get to know about the shading points; you will then be able to see what they are like when finished.

B

PLATE IV.

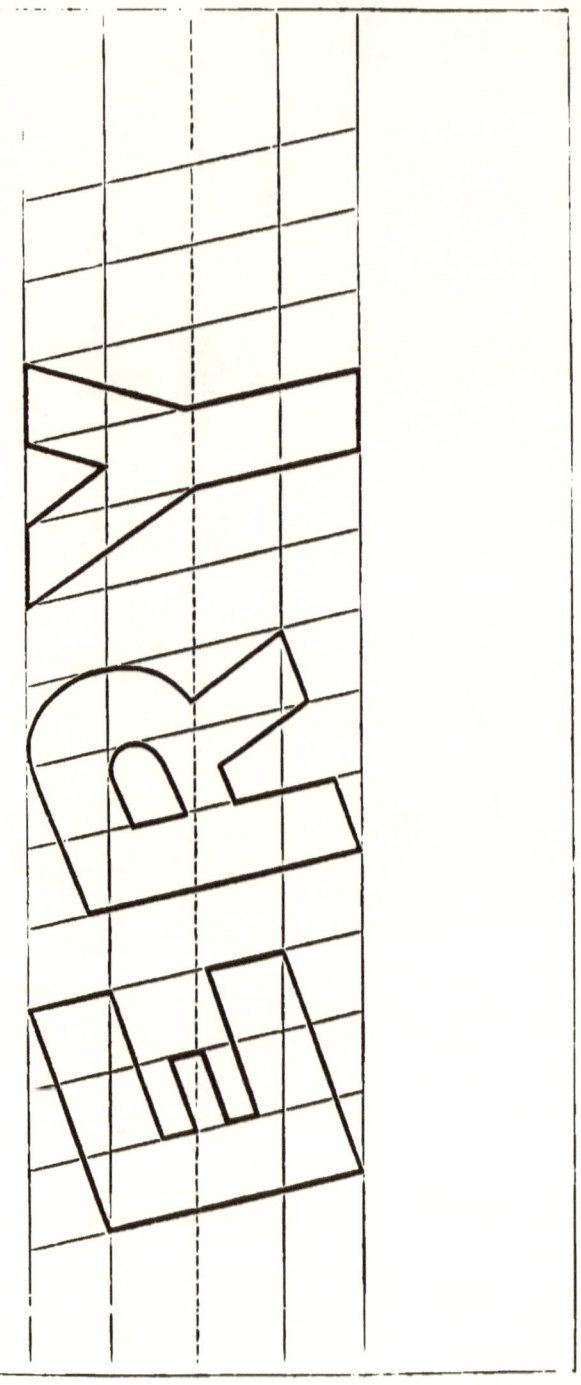

Letters Thrown Back.

PLATE IV. shows the plain letter thrown back. It is done, as you will perceive, by throwing the lines forward at the bottom; that is, by missing the first space at the bottom. By drawing a third or middle line the same distance from the second as the second is from the first, you get the starting-point for the "lay" of your letter. It is plainly shown in the plate. Of course they can as easily be thrown forward as backward, by simply reversing your lines. It is a letter that will be often found useful; at any rate it is as well to know how to make them when required.

Various Kinds of Letters.

PLATE V. is produced from the same points as the other letters. By a very short study you will easily find where they begin and end; in fact they are the easiest to do. You have merely to divide by the number of your letters, and if you keep them plumb you are right; but you will be none the worse for practising them for a time by the system.

PLATE V.

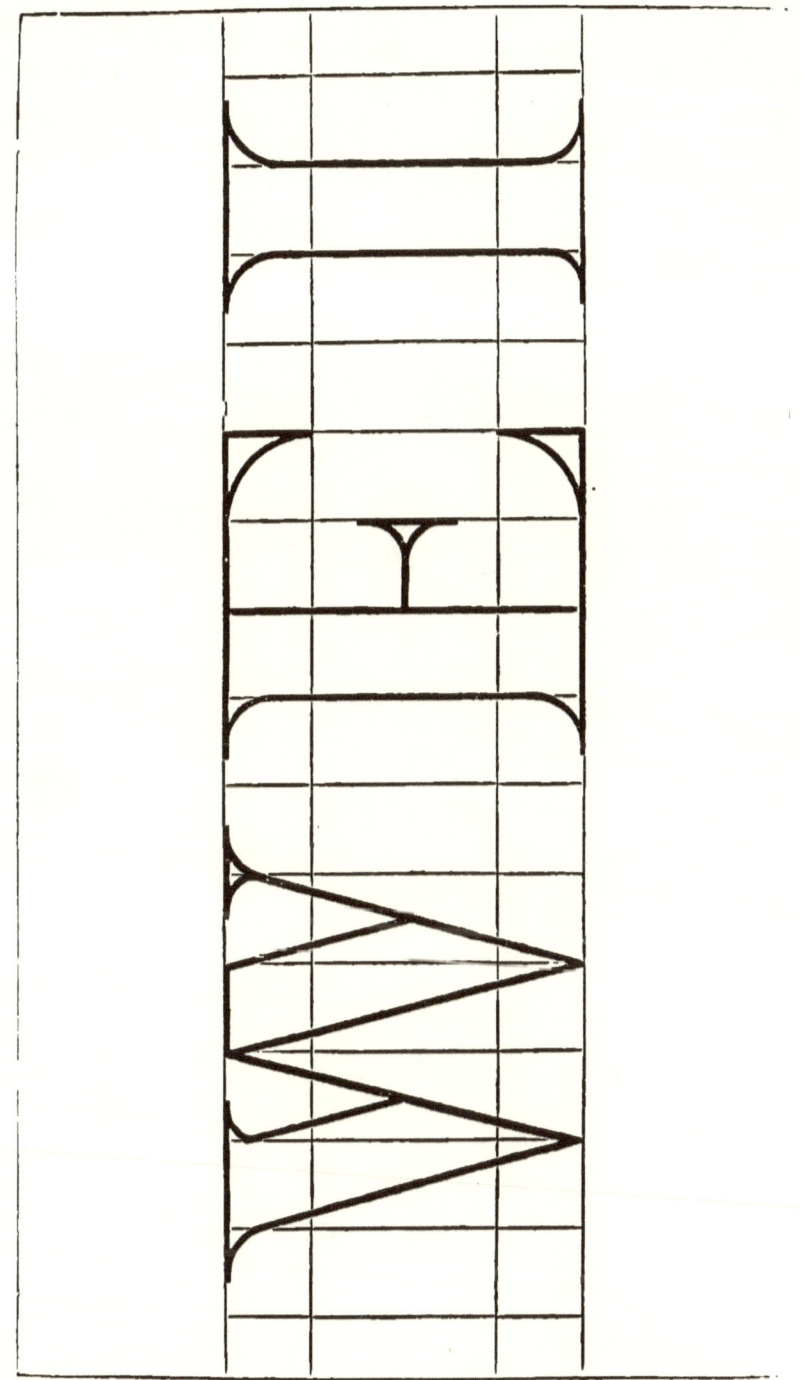

PLATE VI.

Extended Letters.

PLATE VI. shows how to make extended letters. It is the same as the other, only leave two spaces for the centre as body of the letter. Another way is to divide your sign into as many spaces, then mark off the thickness for the two outsides of the letters.

If you want a space between, you must of course allow for it, as it is easy to extend until you get out of all proportion. The thickness of the letter is simply a matter of taste.

Having now given you all the information required for the construction of what may be called the plain or unshaded letter, I will proceed to show you how to get the shading points. But before doing so I would here strongly recommend the pupil to try his hand at perspective, so that he may be able to "raise" the letters, in order to make them look as if cut out of the solid. For this purpose he can do nothing better than to get "Davidson on House Painting,"* in which there are lessons specially adapted to his wants, together with many hints that will be useful and profitable to him as a house painter. The lessons will be found to be easy to follow, as there are but few of them; besides, they are so simple that they can be understood by any one, even should he be altogether unacquainted with perspective.

* Published by Crosby Lockwood & Son.

PLATE VII.

Shaded Letters.

PLATE VII. A shaded S. I have drawn S in preference to other letters, first because it is so difficult to make, and also because in many cases the shading is botched, even by good hands.

Now take a good look at it. Is it not far preferable to what you generally see as you go along the streets, such as the small one in the plate, which I submit is a fair sample as to shape of the ordinary S seen on most signs? It looks as if it were making an apology for its maker—as if it said, "I am ashamed of myself, but he could not make me any better." Take the other made on this system; you cannot, I think, mend the turn of the ends nor get a bolder letter. It challenges the eye, and seems to say, "Look at me, beat me if you can." The shading points are seen at a glance, and I do not see that I need describe them, as they are quite plain enough.

PLATE VIII. E. I have made these plates large, as I want the pupil to be able to see at a glance and to understand the points, shape, and style of the letters; and he will do that far better if he can get a decided view of them, than if I were to make them small and cramped, which might leave him in doubt.

Here you have what I take to be the nicest of the square letters. It does not need much description —it is as "plain as a pike-staff;" the shading points are easy to be seen. But with regard to the manner of colouring the shade, I think I had better leave that alone, simply remarking that two distinct shades of the same colour are necessary, and if properly selected, with a lighter colour for the strong lights, the effect will be—well, just as you make it.

Should you want a back shade, make it a darker shade of the ground colour if possible.

The letter here represented may not suit your

PLATE VIII.

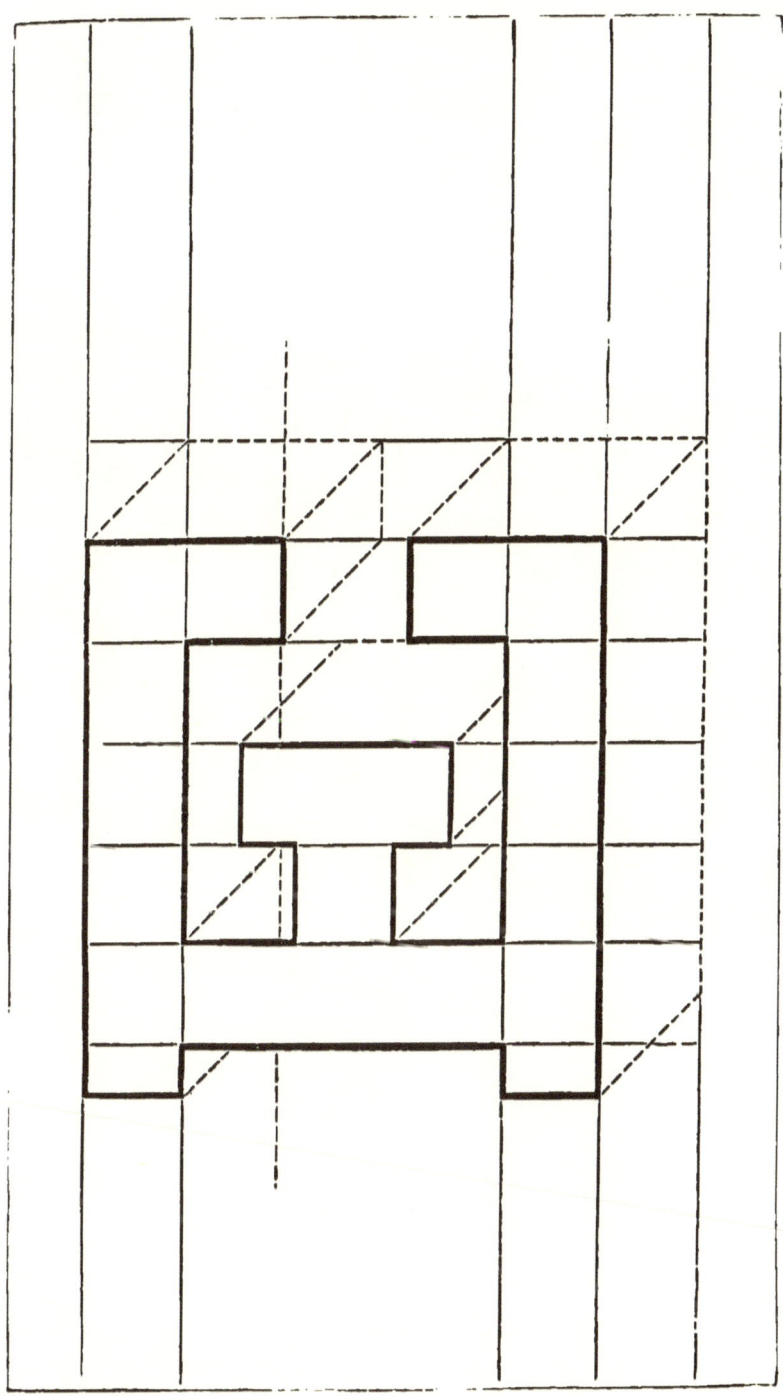

taste or idea of what you would like to see; but you must remember that you are not to make your letters all your life by my model; only learn how to make yours from mine, and, as I said before, get a style of your own. There is room enough and scope enough for you to become an artist; for, believe me, there is a vast amount of skill and taste to be displayed in letter painting, and, what may be better still, there is money to be made by it, yea, and there is inside work in bad weather with less heavy labour to be undergone. Believe me, it is worth learning for very many reasons, the least of which I have stated here. You can always get a job, and a better wage. Think of these things and persevere.

PLATE IX. The next is the letter R. I have preferred to give you what is generally considered the worst to do, but really I cannot find that with the "system" one letter is worse to make than another. They are so plainly laid out by the squares that you might very well say they are all squares.

Here you have R extended, and thicker or more massive than the other; in fact, the variety is endless to which the system is applicable. I do not know of any letter but may be done by it, with a little thought. I have done all sorts, both old and new styles; but I seldom use it now. I just say 5 out of 20 (inches) or 12 out of 50 (feet or inches), as the case may be ; having found the number that it will go, I place my compasses to my rule, dot it off on the sign, draw one straight

PLATE IX.

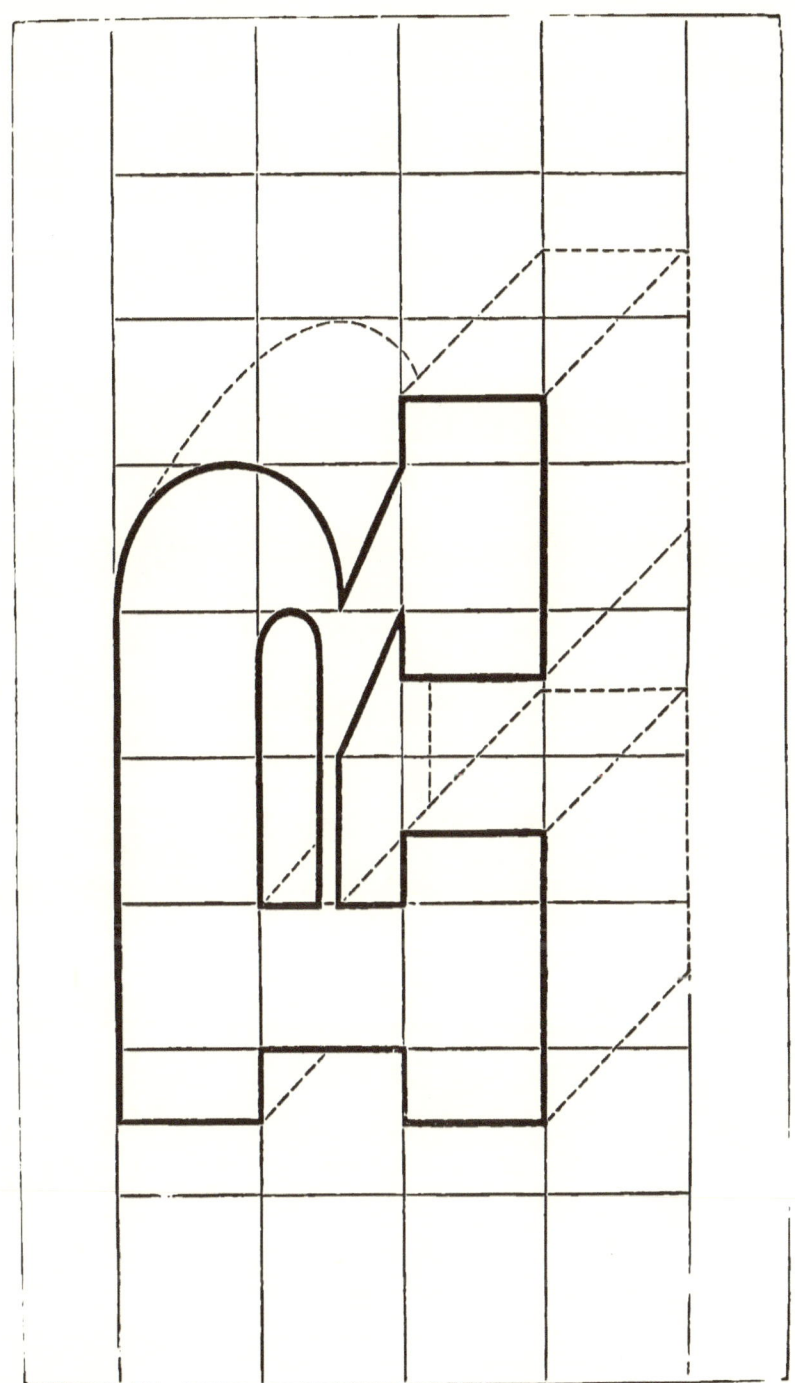

line to keep the letter plumb, take my brush, and off I go.

But if I meet with an S, and if a very particular job, I will draw the spaces for that letter, but not always. Only there is this in it—if you are up a ladder it saves your getting down to look at your work, and possibly having it to alter. With the system that is not necessary, as you cannot miss your mark. For shade and style, of course it is natural that you should want a " see " when you have finished ; but all the seeing in the world will not alter the affair when you make it right to begin with, which the system does.

PLATE X. is universally proclaimed as a bad one. Well, try if you can do it. Here it is; look at it, the terror is gone. It is as simple as painting the back of a shutter, better pay, and not half such hard work. It is made by the same rule. There are two of them; make them, and there is nothing to hinder a dozen different sorts.

PLATE X.

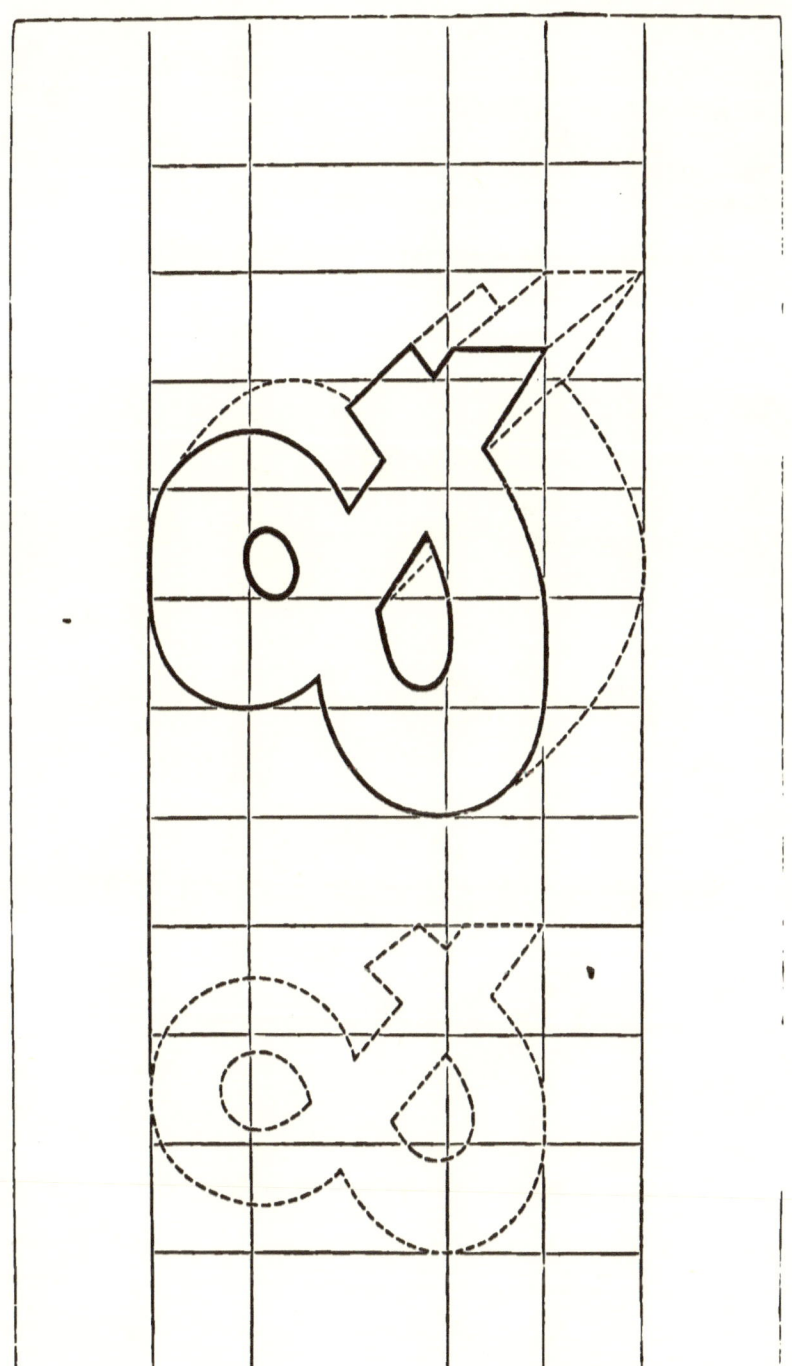

C

PLATE XI.

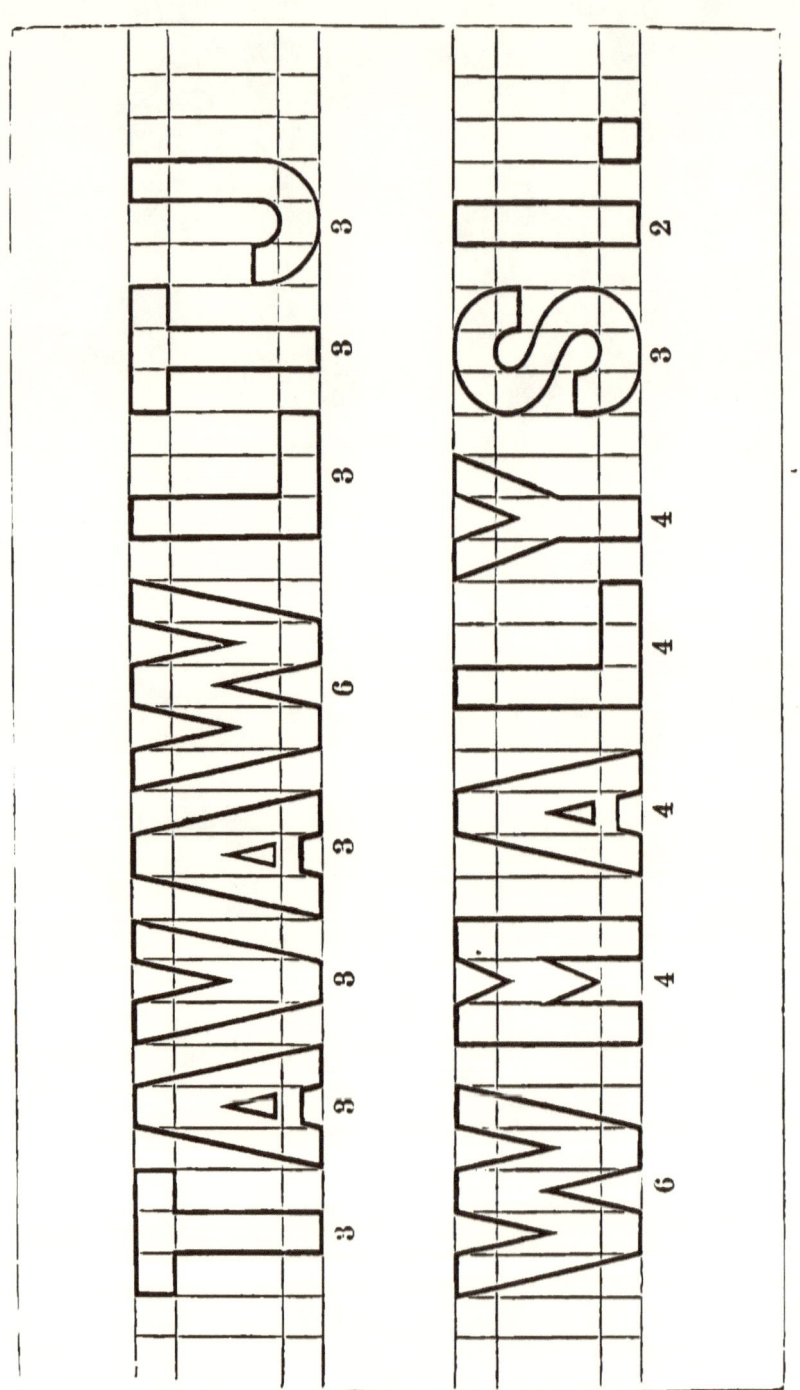

PLATE XI. Here you have a few examples to show the way the letters sometimes run into each other, so as to take up less room or fewer spaces, by observing which you may avoid mistakes when you come to actual practice. Take notice of the first two letters, T and A, A and V, and so on to the end of the line of eight letters ; while the under line has only seven letters, of the same size, but taking up the same space. But by a rough scrat or two with your pencil, as shown on Plate I., you can always tell to a nicety how many divisions you will want.

PLATE XII. is simply to show one or two ways by which the system may be made useful in making fancy letters without any extra trouble in the sketching. No doubt the pupil will soon be able to find innumerable ways and styles for himself.

PLATE XII.

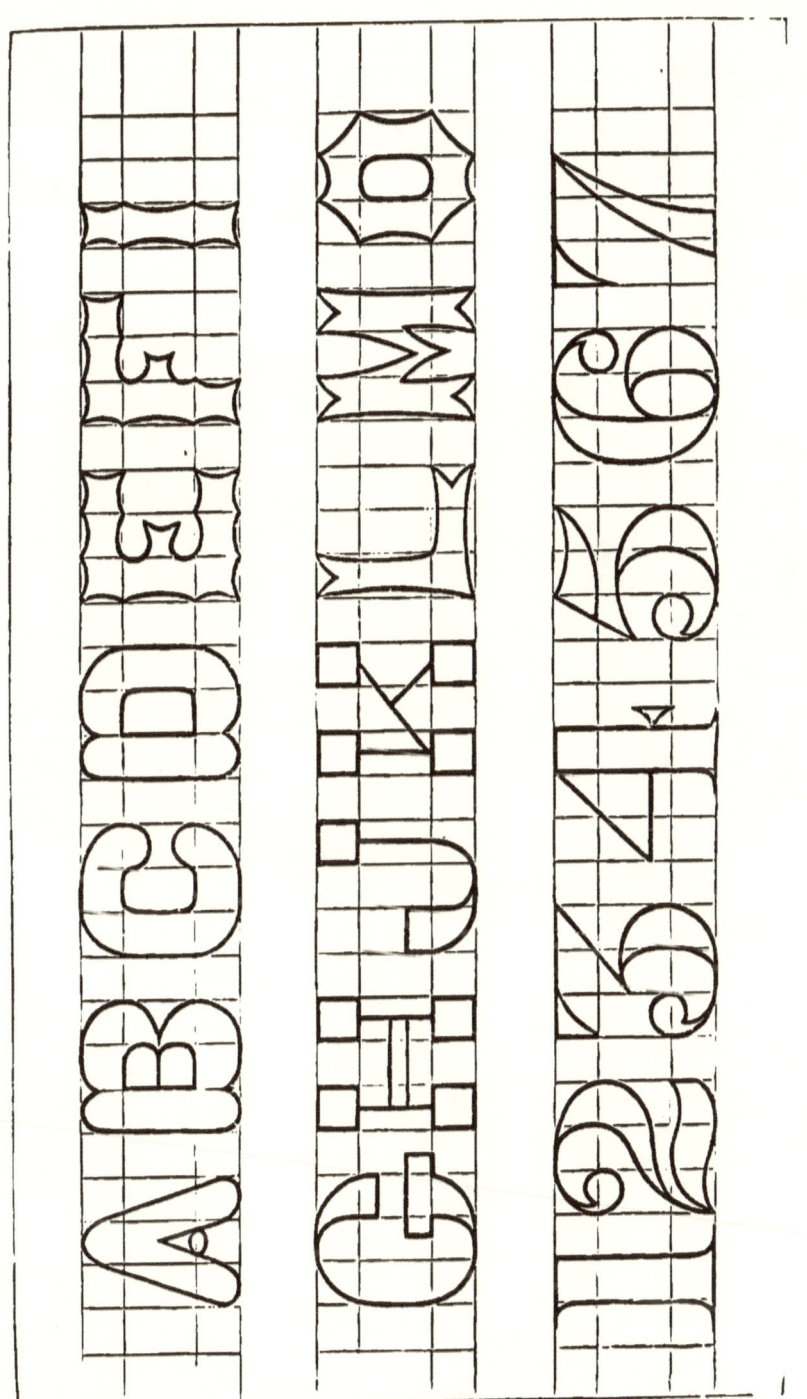

Circle or Scroll Work.

I may here mention that the system is equally applicable to circle or scroll work. You may find your spaces on either by simply dividing the circle or scroll by your dividers; or you may draw a straight line underneath, divide that, and carry it on to your circle or scroll by your straight-edge.

One way for making your letters proportionate in or on a circle is to divide the inner and outer edges of the circle separately ; or you may do it by dividing the inner edge and putting in a centre point—a pin will do—and by keeping your straight edge to that, and bringing it to your division, drawing the line from edge to edge of the circle, your letter will be proportionate. As the outer edge is larger it occupies a greater space; it therefore follows that your letters should be rather thicker or heavier at the outer edge, and this plan gives the exact thing required, and makes, if well done, a very pretty letter which looks well. And why it should not be well done I do not know, as the system if steadily followed will let it be nothing else than well done; only cut in the lines clean with your brush, and if you are not a good letter writer and painter in a month—then I say you have not tried as you ought to have done.

Concluding Remarks.

In conclusion, I will just tell you that when I was not more than sixteen years old I was offered twenty-six shillings a week as sign painter. No one knew how I got at it, and I never told any one, but I will tell it now. I had work to do at which I had to sit very still; and in time, although it was work that was very fine, I got with practice that I could do it with my eyes shut and without thinking about it. That being the case I was sorely puzzled to keep myself awake. I had nothing at all to look at but a lot of show-bills, and I counted the letters on them until I was many a time sick of the job.

At last I counted the legs and spaces of the letters until I found out this system. I tried it, and found it to answer admirably. I did my spacing at home and made notes of my distances on slips of paper; and when I went to the shop the men thought I must be a genius. I knew the ground I had to work on; I spaced it at home, as I have said; when I got to the shop I set my compasses to my rule, snapped my lines lengthways, and *never* made a mistake. If I did it was at home, and no one ever saw it; so, like many another, I got credit for a genius I never possessed. Go ye and do likewise.

PRINTED BY J. S. VIRTUE AND CO., LIMITED, CITY ROAD, LONDON.

WEALE'S RUDIMENTARY SCIENTIFIC SERIES.

Capio Lumen

*** The volumes of this Series are freely Illustrated with Woodcuts, or otherwise, where requisite. Throughout the following List it must be understood that the books are bound in limp cloth, unless otherwise stated; *but the volumes marked with a ‡ may also be had strongly bound in cloth boards for 6d. extra.*

N.B.—In ordering from this List it is recommended, as a means of facilitating business and obviating error, to quote the numbers affixed to the volumes, as well as the titles and prices.

CIVIL ENGINEERING, SURVEYING, ETC.

No.
31. *WELLS AND WELL-SINKING.* By JOHN GEO. SWINDELL, A.R.I.B.A., and G. R. BURNELL, C.E. Revised Edition. With a New Appendix on the Qualities of Water. Illustrated. 2s.

35. *THE BLASTING AND QUARRYING OF STONE,* for Building and other Purposes. With Remarks on the Blowing up of Bridges. By Gen. Sir JOHN BURGOYNE, Bart., K.C.B. Illustrated. 1s. 6d.

43. *TUBULAR, AND OTHER IRON GIRDER BRIDGES,* particularly describing the Britannia and Conway Tubular Bridges. By G. DRYSDALE DEMPSEY, C.E. Fourth Edition. 2s.

44. *FOUNDATIONS AND CONCRETE WORKS,* with Practical Remarks on Footings, Sand, Concrete, Béton, Pile-driving, Caissons, and Cofferdams, &c. By E. DOBSON. Fifth Edition. 1s. 6d.

60. *LAND AND ENGINEERING SURVEYING.* By T. BAKER, C.E. Fourteenth Edition, revised by Professor J. R. YOUNG. 2s.‡

80*. *EMBANKING LANDS FROM THE SEA.* With examples and Particulars of actual Embankments, &c. By J. WIGGINS, F.G.S. 2s.

81. *WATER WORKS,* for the Supply of Cities and Towns. With a Description of the Principal Geological Formations of England as influencing Supplies of Water; and Details of Engines and Pumping Machinery for raising Water. By SAMUEL HUGHES, F.G.S., C.E. New Edition. 4s.‡

118. *CIVIL ENGINEERING IN NORTH AMERICA,* a Sketch of. By DAVID STEVENSON, F.R.S.E., &c. Plates and Diagrams. 3s.

167. *IRON BRIDGES, GIRDERS, ROOFS, AND OTHER* WORKS. By FRANCIS CAMPIN, C.E. 2s. 6d.‡

197. *ROADS AND STREETS (THE CONSTRUCTION OF).* By HENRY LAW, C.E., revised and enlarged by D. K. CLARK, C.E., including pavements of Stone, Wood, Asphalte, &c. 4s. 6d.‡

203. *SANITARY WORK IN THE SMALLER TOWNS AND IN* VILLAGES. By C. SLAGG, A.M.I.C.E. Revised Edition. 3s.‡

212. *GAS-WORKS, THEIR CONSTRUCTION AND ARRANGE-MENT;* and the Manufacture and Distribution of Coal Gas. Originally written by SAMUEL HUGHES, C.E. Re-written and enlarged by WILLIAM RICHARDS, C.E. Seventh Edition, with important additions. 5s. 6d.‡

213. *PIONEER ENGINEERING.* A Treatise on the Engineering Operations connected with the Settlement of Waste Lands in New Countries. By EDWARD DOBSON, Assoc. Inst. C.E. 4s. 6d.‡

216. *MATERIALS AND CONSTRUCTION;* A Theoretical and Practical Treatise on the Strains, Designing, and Erection of Works of Construction. By FRANCIS CAMPIN, C.E. Second Edition, revised. 3s.‡

219. *CIVIL ENGINEERING.* By HENRY LAW, M.Inst. C.E. Including HYDRAULIC ENGINEERING by GEO. R. BURNELL, M.Inst. C.E. Seventh Edition, revised, with large additions by D. KINNEAR CLARK, M.Inst. C.E. 6s. 6d., Cloth boards, 7s. 6d.

☞ *The ‡ indicates that these vols. may be had strongly bound at 6d. extra.*

LONDON : CROSBY LOCKWOOD AND SON,

MECHANICAL ENGINEERING, ETC.

33. *CRANES*, the Construction of, and other Machinery for Raising Heavy Bodies. By JOSEPH GLYNN, F.R.S. Illustrated. 1s. 6d.
34. *THE STEAM ENGINE.* By Dr. LARDNER. Illustrated. 1s. 6d.
59. *STEAM BOILERS:* their Construction and Management. By R. ARMSTRONG, C.E. Illustrated. 1s. 6d.
82. *THE POWER OF WATER*, as applied to drive Flour Mills, and to give motion to Turbines, &c. By JOSEPH GLYNN, F.R.S. 2s.‡
98. *PRACTICAL MECHANISM*, the Elements of; and Machine Tools. By T. BAKER, C.E. With Additions by J. NASMYTH, C.E. 2s. 6d.‡
139. *THE STEAM ENGINE*, a Treatise on the Mathematical Theory of, with Rules and Examples for Practical Men. By T. BAKER, C.E. 1s. 6d.
164. *MODERN WORKSHOP PRACTICE*, as applied to Steam Engines, Bridges, Ship-building, Cranes, &c. By J. G. WINTON. Fourth Edition, much enlarged and carefully revised. 3s. 6d.‡ [*Just published.*
165. *IRON AND HEAT*, exhibiting the Principles concerned in the Construction of Iron Beams, Pillars, and Girders. By J. ARMOUR. 2s. 6d.‡
166. *POWER IN MOTION:* Horse-Power, Toothed-Wheel Gearing, Long and Short Driving Bands, and Angular Forces. By J. ARMOUR. 2s.‡
171. *THE WORKMAN'S MANUAL OF ENGINEERING DRAWING.* By J. MAXTON. 6th Edn. With 7 Plates and 350 Cuts. 3s. 6d.‡
190. *STEAM AND THE STEAM ENGINE*, Stationary and Portable. Being an Extension of the Elementary Treatise on the Steam Engine of Mr. JOHN SEWELL. By D. K. CLARK, M.I.C.E. 3s. 6d.‡
200. *FUEL*, its Combustion and Economy. By C. W. WILLIAMS With Recent Practice in the Combustion and Economy of Fuel—Coal, Coke Wood, Peat, Petroleum, &c.—by D. K. CLARK, M.I.C.E. 3s. 6d.‡
202. *LOCOMOTIVE ENGINES.* By G. D. DEMPSEY, C.E.; with large additions by D. KINNEAR CLARK, M.I.C.E. 3s.‡
211. *THE BOILERMAKER'S ASSISTANT* in Drawing, Templating, and Calculating Boiler and Tank Work. By JOHN COURTNEY, Practical Boiler Maker. Edited by D. K. CLARK, C.E. 100 Illustrations. 2s.
217. *SEWING MACHINERY:* Its Construction, History, &c., with full Technical Directions for Adjusting, &c. By J. W. URQUHART, C.E. 2s.‡
223. *MECHANICAL ENGINEERING.* Comprising Metallurgy, Moulding, Casting, Forging, Tools, Workshop Machinery, Manufacture of the Steam Engine, &c. By FRANCIS CAMPIN, C.E. Second Edition. 2s. 6d.‡
236. *DETAILS OF MACHINERY.* Comprising Instructions for the Execution of various Works in Iron. By FRANCIS CAMPIN, C.E. 3s.‡
237. *THE SMITHY AND FORGE;* including the Farrier's Art and Coach Smithing. By W. J. E. CRANE. Illustrated. 2s. 6d.‡
238. *THE SHEET-METAL WORKER'S GUIDE;* a Practical Handbook for Tinsmiths, Coppersmiths, Zincworkers, &c. With 94 Diagrams and Working Patterns. By W. J. E. CRANE. Second Edition, revised. 1s. 5d.
251. *STEAM AND MACHINERY MANAGEMENT:* with Hints on Construction and Selection. By M. POWIS BALE, M.I.M.E. 2s. 6d.‡
254. *THE BOILERMAKER'S READY-RECKONER.* By J. COURTNEY. Edited by D. K. CLARK, C.E. 4s., limp; 5s., half-bound.
255. *LOCOMOTIVE ENGINE-DRIVING.* A Practical Manual for Engineers in charge of Locomotive Engines. By MICHAEL REYNOLDS, M.S.E. Eighth Edition. 3s. 6d., limp; 4s. 6d. cloth boards.
256. *STATIONARY ENGINE-DRIVING.* A Practical Manual for Engineers in charge of Stationary Engines. By MICHAEL REYNOLDS, M.S.E. Third Edition. 3s. 6d. limp; 4s. 6d. cloth boards.
260. *IRON BRIDGES OF MODERATE SPAN:* their Construction and Erection. By HAMILTON W. PENDRED, C.E. 2s.

☞ *The ‡ indicates that these vols. may be had strongly bound at 6d. extra.*

7, STATIONERS' HALL COURT, LUDGATE HILL, E.C.

MINING, METALLURGY, ETC.

4. *MINERALOGY*, Rudiments of; a concise View of the General Properties of Minerals. By A. RAMSAY, F.G.S., F.R.G.S., &c. Third Edition, revised and enlarged. Illustrated. 3s. 6d.‡

117. *SUBTERRANEOUS SURVEYING*, with and without the Magnetic Needle. By T. FENWICK and T. BAKER, C.E. Illustrated. 2s. 6d. ‡

133. *METALLURGY OF COPPER ;* an Introduction to the Methods of Seeking, Mining, and Assaying Copper. By R. H. LAMBORN. 2s. 6d. ‡

135. *ELECTRO-METALLURGY;* Practically Treated. By ALEXANDER WATT. Ninth Edition, enlarged and revised, with additional Illustrations, and including the most recent Processes. 3s. 6d.‡

172. *MINING TOOLS*, Manual of. For the Use of Mine Managers, Agents, Students, &c. By WILLIAM MORGANS. 2s. 6d.

172*. *MINING TOOLS, ATLAS* of Engravings to Illustrate the above, containing 235 Illustrations, drawn to Scale. 4to. 4s. 6d.

176. *METALLURGY OF IRON.* Containing History of Iron Manufacture, Methods of Assay, and Analyses of Iron Ores, Processes of Manufacture of Iron and Steel, &c. By H. BAUERMAN, F.G.S. Fifth Edition, revised and enlarged. 5s.‡

180. *COAL AND COAL MINING.* By WARINGTON W. SMYTH, M.A., F.R.S. Sixth Edition, revised 3s. 6d.‡

195. *THE MINERAL SURVEYOR AND VALUER'S COMPLETE GUIDE.* Comprising a Treatise on Improved Mining Surveying and the Valuation of Mining Properties, with new Traverse Tables. By W. LINTERN, Mining Engineer. Second Edition, with an Appendix on Magnetic and Angular Surveying. With Four Plates. 3s. 6d.‡ [*Just published.*

214. *SLATE AND SLATE QUARRYING*, Scientific, Practical, and Commercial. By D. C. DAVIES, F.G.S., Mining Engineer, &c. 3s.‡

264. *A FIRST BOOK OF MINING AND QUARRYING*, with the Sciences connected therewith, for Primary Schools and Self-Instruction. By J. H. COLLINS, F.G.S. Second Edition, with additions. 1s. 6d.

ARCHITECTURE, BUILDING, ETC.

16. *ARCHITECTURE—ORDERS*—The Orders and their Æsthetic Principles. By W. H. LEEDS. Illustrated. 1s. 6d.

17. *ARCHITECTURE—STYLES*—The History and Description of the Styles of Architecture of Various Countries, from the Earliest to the Present Period. By T. TALBOT BURY, F.R.I.B.A., &c. Illustrated. 2s. *⁎⁎ ORDERS AND STYLES OF ARCHITECTURE, in One Vol., 3s. 6d,*

18. *ARCHITECTURE—DESIGN*—The Principles of Design in Architecture, as deducible from Nature and exemplified in the Works of the Greek and Gothic Architects. By E. L. GARBETT, Architect. Illustrated. 2s.6d.
⁎⁎ *The three preceding Works, in One handsome Vol., half bound, entitled "MODERN ARCHITECTURE," price 6s.*

22. *THE ART OF BUILDING*, Rudiments of. General Principles of Construction, Materials used in Building, Strength and Use of Materials, Working Drawings, Specifications, and Estimates. By E. DOBSON, 2s.‡

25. *MASONRY AND STONECUTTING :* Rudimentary Treatise on the Principles of Masonic Projection and their application to Construction. By EDWARD DOBSON, M.R.I.B.A., &c. 2s. 6d.‡

42. *COTTAGE BUILDING.* By C. BRUCE ALLEN, Architect. Tenth Edition, revised and enlarged. With a Chapter on Economic Cottages for Allotments, by EDWARD E. ALLEN, C.E. 2s.

45. *LIMES, CEMENTS, MORTARS, CONCRETES, MASTICS,* PLASTERING, &c. By G. R. BURNELL, C.E. Thirteenth Edition. 1s. 6d.

The ‡ indicates that these vols. may be had strongly bound at 6d. extra.

LONDON : CROSBY LOCKWOOD AND SON,

Architecture, Building, etc., *continued.*

57. *WARMING AND VENTILATION.* An Exposition of the General Principles as applied to Domestic and Public Buildings, Mines, Lighthouses, Ships, &c. By C. TOMLINSON, F.R.S., &c. Illustrated. 3s.

111. *ARCHES, PIERS, BUTTRESSES, &c.*: Experimental Essays on the Principles of Construction. By W. BLAND. Illustrated. 1s. 6d.

116. *THE ACOUSTICS OF PUBLIC BUILDINGS;* or, The Principles of the Science of Sound applied to the purposes of the Architect and Builder. By T. ROGER SMITH, M.R.I.B.A., Architect. Illustrated. 1s. 6d.

127. *ARCHITECTURAL MODELLING IN PAPER,* the Art of. By T. A. RICHARDSON, Architect. Illustrated. 1s. 6d.

128. *VITRUVIUS—THE ARCHITECTURE OF MARCUS VITRUVIUS POLLO.* In Ten Books. Translated from the Latin by JOSEPH GWILT, F.S.A., F.R.A.S. With 23 Plates. 5s.

130. *GRECIAN ARCHITECTURE,* An Inquiry into the Principles of Beauty in; with an Historical View of the Rise and Progress of the Art in Greece. By the EARL OF ABERDEEN. 1s.

. *The two preceding Works in One handsome Vol., half bound, entitled* "ANCIENT ARCHITECTURE," *price 6s.*

132. *THE ERECTION OF DWELLING-HOUSES.* Illustrated by a Perspective View, Plans, Elevations, and Sections of a pair of Semi-detached Villas, with the Specification, Quantities, and Estimates, &c. By S. H. BROOKS. New Edition, with Plates. 2s. 6d.‡

156. *QUANTITIES & MEASUREMENTS* in Bricklayers', Masons', Plasterers', Plumbers', Painters', Paperhangers', Gilders', Smiths', Carpenters' and Joiners' Work. By A. C. BEATON, Surveyor. New Edition. 1s. 6d.

175. *LOCKWOOD & SON'S BUILDER'S & CONTRACTOR'S* PRICE BOOK, containing the latest Prices of all kinds of Builders' Materials and Labour, and of all Trades connected with Building, &c., &c. Edited by F. T. W. MILLER, Architect. Published annually. 3s. 6d. ; half bound, 4s.

182. *CARPENTRY AND JOINERY—*THE ELEMENTARY PRINCIPLES OF CARPENTRY. Chiefly composed from the Standard Work of THOMAS TREDGOLD, C.E. With a TREATISE ON JOINERY by E. WYNDHAM TARN, M.A. Fourth Edition, Revised. 3s. 6d.‡

182*. *CARPENTRY AND JOINERY.* ATLAS of 35 Plates to accompany the above. With Descriptive Letterpress. 4to. 6s.

185. *THE COMPLETE MEASURER ;* the Measurement of Boards, Glass, &c.; Unequal-sided, Square-sided, Octagonal-sided, Round Timber and Stone, and Standing Timber, &c. By RICHARD HORTON. Fifth Edition. 4s. ; strongly bound in leather, 5s.

187. *HINTS TO YOUNG ARCHITECTS.* By G. WIGHTWICK. New Edition. By G. H. GUILLAUME. Illustrated. 3s. 6d.‡

188. *HOUSE PAINTING, GRAINING, MARBLING, AND SIGN WRITING :* with a Course of Elementary Drawing for House-Painters, Sign-Writers, &c., and a Collection of Useful Receipts. By ELLIS A. DAVIDSON. Fifth Edition. With Coloured Plates. 5s. cloth limp; 6s. cloth boards.

189. *THE RUDIMENTS OF PRACTICAL BRICKLAYING.* In Six Sections: General Principles; Arch Drawing, Cutting, and Setting; Pointing; Paving, Tiling, Materials; Slating and Plastering; Practical Geometry, Mensuration, &c. By ADAM HAMMOND. Sixth Edition. 1s. 6d.

191. *PLUMBING.* A Text-Book to the Practice of the Art or Craft of the Plumber. With Chapters upon House Drainage and Ventilation. Fifth Edition. With 380 Illustrations. By W. P. BUCHAN. 3s. 6d.‡

192. *THE TIMBER IMPORTER'S, TIMBER MERCHANT'S,* and BUILDER'S STANDARD GUIDE. By R. E. GRANDY. 2s.

206. *A BOOK ON BUILDING, Civil and Ecclesiastical,* including CHURCH RESTORATION. With the Theory of Domes and the Great Pyramid, &c. By Sir EDMUND BECKETT, Bart., LL.D., Q.C., F.R.A.S. 4s. 6d.‡

☞ *The ‡ indicates that these vols. may be had strongly bound at 6d. extra.*

Architecture, Building, etc., *continued.*

226. *THE JOINTS MADE AND USED BY BUILDERS* in the Construction of various kinds of Engineering and Architectural Works. By WYVILL J. CHRISTY, Architect. With upwards of 160 Engravings on Wood. 3s.‡

228. *THE CONSTRUCTION OF ROOFS OF WOOD AND IRON.* By E. WYNDHAM TARN, M.A., Architect. Second Edition, revised. 1s. 6d.

229. *ELEMENTARY DECORATION:* as applied to the Interior and Exterior Decoration of Dwelling-Houses, &c. By J. W. FACEY. 2s.

257. *PRACTICAL HOUSE DECORATION.* A Guide to the Art of Ornamental Painting. By JAMES W. FACEY. 2s. 6d.

** *The two preceding Works, in One handsome Vol., half-bound, entitled* "HOUSE DECORATION, ELEMENTARY AND PRACTICAL," *price* 5s.

230. *HANDRAILING.* Showing New and Simple Methods for finding the Pitch of the Plank. Drawing the Moulds, Bevelling, Jointing-up, and Squaring the Wreath. By GEORGE COLLINGS. Plates and Diagrams. 1s. 6d.

247. *BUILDING ESTATES:* a Rudimentary Treatise on the Development, Sale, Purchase, and General Management of Building Land. By FOWLER MAITLAND, Surveyor. Second Edition, revised. 2s.

248. *PORTLAND CEMENT FOR USERS.* By HENRY FAIJA, Assoc. M. Inst. C.E. Second Edition, corrected. Illustrated. 2s.

252. *BRICKWORK:* a Practical Treatise, embodying the General and Higher Principles of Bricklaying, Cutting and Setting, &c. By F. WALKER. Second Edition, Revised and Enlarged. 1s. 6d.

23. *THE PRACTICAL BRICK AND TILE BOOK.* Comprising:
189. BRICK AND TILE MAKING, by E. DOBSON, A.I.C.E.; PRACTICAL BRICKLAY-
252. ING, by A. HAMMOND; BRICKWORK, by F. WALKER. 550 pp. with 270 Illustrations. 6s. Strongly half-bound.

253. *THE TIMBER MERCHANT'S, SAW-MILLER'S, AND* IMPORTER'S FREIGHT-BOOK AND ASSISTANT. By WM. RICHARDSON. With a Chapter on Speeds of Saw-Mill Machinery, &c. By M. POWIS BALE, A.M.Inst.C.E. 3s.‡

258. *CIRCULAR WORK IN CARPENTRY AND JOINERY.* A Practical Treatise on Circular Work of Single and Double Curvature. By GEORGE COLLINGS, Author of "A Treatise on Handrailing." 2s. 6d.

259. *GAS FITTING:* A Practical Handbook treating of every Description of Gas Laying and Fitting. By JOHN BLACK. With 122 Illustrations. 2s. 6d.‡

261. *SHORING AND ITS APPLICATION:* A Handbook for the Use of Students. By GEORGE H. BLAGROVE. 1s. 6d.   [*Just published.*

265. *THE ART OF PRACTICAL BRICK CUTTING AND* SETTING. By ADAM HAMMOND, Author of "Practical Bricklaying." With 90 Engravings. 1s. 6d.   [*Just Published.*

SHIPBUILDING, NAVIGATION, MARINE ENGINEERING, ETC.

51. *NAVAL ARCHITECTURE.* An Exposition of the Elementary Principles of the Science, and their Practical Application to Naval Construction. By J. PEAKE. Fifth Edition, with Plates and Diagrams. 3s. 6d.‡

53*. *SHIPS FOR OCEAN & RIVER SERVICE*, Elementary and Practical Principles of the Construction of. By H. A. SOMMERFELDT. 1s. 6d.

53**. *AN ATLAS OF ENGRAVINGS* to Illustrate the above. Twelve large folding plates. Royal 4to, cloth. 7s. 6d.

54. *MASTING, MAST-MAKING, AND RIGGING OF SHIPS*, Also Tables of Spars, Rigging, Blocks; Chain, Wire, and Hemp Ropes, &c., relative to every class of vessels. By ROBERT KIPPING, N.A. 2s.

54*. *IRON SHIP-BUILDING.* With Practical Examples and Details. By JOHN GRANTHAM, C.E. 5th Edition. 4s.

The ‡ indicates that these vols. may be had strongly bound at 6d. extra.

Shipbuilding, Navigation, Marine Engineering, etc., *cont.*

55. *THE SAILOR'S SEA BOOK:* a Rudimentary Treatise on Navigation. By JAMES GREENWOOD, B.A. With numerous Woodcuts and Coloured Plates. New and enlarged edition. By W. H. ROSSER. 2s. 6d.‡

80. *MARINE ENGINES AND STEAM VESSELS.* By ROBERT MURRAY, C.E. Eighth Edition, thoroughly Revised, with Additions by the Author and by GEORGE CARLISLE, C.E., Senior Surveyor to the Board of Trade, Liverpool. 4s. 6d. limp; 5s. cloth boards.

83*bis*. *THE FORMS OF SHIPS AND BOATS.* By W. BLAND. Seventh Edition, Revised, with numerous Illustrations and Models. 1s. 6d.

99. *NAVIGATION AND NAUTICAL ASTRONOMY,* in Theory and Practice. By Prof. J. R. YOUNG. New Edition. 2s. 6d.

106. *SHIPS' ANCHORS,* a Treatise on. By G. COTSELL, N.A. 1s. 6d.

149. *SAILS AND SAIL-MAKING.* With Draughting, and the Centre of Effort of the Sails; Weights and Sizes of Ropes; Masting, Rigging, and Sails of Steam Vessels, &c. 12th Edition. By R. KIPPING. N.A.. 2s. 6d.‡

155. *ENGINEER'S GUIDE TO THE ROYAL & MERCANTILE NAVIES.* By a PRACTICAL ENGINEER. Revised by D. F. M'CARTHY. 3s.

55 & 204. *PRACTICAL NAVIGATION.* Consisting of The Sailor's Sea-Book. By JAMES GREENWOOD and W. H. ROSSER. Together with the requisite Mathematical and Nautical Tables for the Working of the Problems. By H. LAW, C.E., and Prof. J. R. YOUNG. 7s. Half-bound.

AGRICULTURE, GARDENING, ETC.

61*. *A COMPLETE READY RECKONER FOR THE ADMEA-SUREMENT OF LAND,* &c. By A. ARMAN. Third Edition, revised and extended by C. NORRIS, Surveyor, Valuer, &c. 2s.

131. *MILLER'S, CORN MERCHANT'S, AND FARMER'S READY RECKONER.* Second Edition, with a Price List of Modern Flour-Mill Machinery, by W. S. HUTTON, C.E. 2s.

140. *SOILS, MANURES, AND CROPS.* (Vol. 1. OUTLINES OF MODERN FARMING.) By R. SCOTT BURN. Woodcuts. 2s.

141. *FARMING & FARMING ECONOMY,* Notes, Historical and Practical, on. (Vol. 2. OUTLINES OF MODERN FARMING.) By R. SCOTT BURN. 3s.

142. *STOCK; CATTLE, SHEEP, AND HORSES.* (Vol. 3. OUTLINES OF MODERN FARMING.) By R. SCOTT BURN. Woodcuts. 2s. 6d.

145. *DAIRY, PIGS, AND POULTRY,* Management of the. By R. SCOTT BURN. (Vol. 4. OUTLINES OF MODERN FARMING.) 2s.

146. *UTILIZATION OF SEWAGE, IRRIGATION, AND RECLAMATION OF WASTE LAND.* (Vol. 5. OUTLINES OF MODERN FARMING.) By R. SCOTT BURN. Woodcuts. 2s. 6d.

** *Nos. 140-1-2-5-6, in One Vol., handsomely half-bound, entitled* "OUTLINES OF MODERN FARMING." By ROBERT SCOTT BURN. *Price 12s.*

177. *FRUIT TREES,* The Scientific and Profitable Culture of. From the French of DU BREUIL. Revised by GEO. GLENNY. 187 Woodcuts. 3s. 6d.‡

198. *SHEEP; THE HISTORY, STRUCTURE, ECONOMY, AND DISEASES OF.* By W. C. SPOONER, M.R.V.C., &c. Fifth Edition, enlarged, including Specimens of New and Improved Breeds. 3s. 6d.‡

201. *KITCHEN GARDENING MADE EASY.* By GEORGE M. F. GLENNY. Illustrated. 1s. 6d.‡

207. *OUTLINES OF FARM MANAGEMENT, and the Organization of Farm Labour.* By R. SCOTT BURN. 2s. 6d.‡

208. *OUTLINES OF LANDED ESTATES MANAGEMENT.* By R. SCOTT BURN. 2s. 6d.‡

** *Nos. 207 & 208 in One Vol., handsomely half-bound, entitled* "OUTLINES OF LANDED ESTATES AND FARM MANAGEMENT." By R. SCOTT BURN. *Price 6s.*

☞ *The ‡ indicates that these vols. may be had strongly bound at 6d. extra.*

7, STATIONERS' HALL COURT, LUDGATE HILL, E.C.

Agriculture, Gardening, etc., *continued*.

209. *THE TREE PLANTER AND PLANT PROPAGATOR.* A Practical Manual on the Propagation of Forest Trees, Fruit Trees, Flowering Shrubs, Flowering Plants, &c. By SAMUEL WOOD. 2s.‡

210. *THE TREE PRUNER.* A Practical Manual on the Pruning of Fruit Trees, including also their Training and Renovation; also the Pruning of Shrubs, Climbers, and Flowering Plants. By SAMUEL WOOD. 2s.‡

⁂ *Nos. 209 & 210 in One Vol., handsomely half-bound, entitled* "THE TREE PLANTER, PROPAGATOR, AND PRUNER." By SAMUEL WOOD. *Price 5s.*

218. *THE HAY AND STRAW MEASURER:* Being New Tables for the Use of Auctioneers, Valuers, Farmers, Hay and Straw Dealers, &c. By JOHN STEELE. Fourth Edition. 2s.

222. *SUBURBAN FARMING.* The Laying-out and Cultivation of Farms, adapted to the Produce of Milk, Butter, and Cheese, Eggs, Poultry, and Pigs. By Prof. JOHN DONALDSON and R. SCOTT BURN. 3s. 6d.‡

231. *THE ART OF GRAFTING AND BUDDING.* By CHARLES BALTET. With Illustrations. 2s. 6d.‡

232. *COTTAGE GARDENING;* or, Flowers, Fruits, and Vegetables for Small Gardens. By E. HOBDAY. 1s. 6d.

233. *GARDEN RECEIPTS.* Edited by CHARLES W. QUIN. 1s. 6d.

234. *MARKET AND KITCHEN GARDENING.* By C. W. SHAW, 'late Editor of "Gardening Illustrated." 3s.‡　　　　　　*[Just published.*

239. *DRAINING AND EMBANKING.* A Practical Treatise, embodying the most recent experience in the Application of Improved Methods. By JOHN SCOTT, late Professor of Agriculture and Rural Economy at the Royal Agricultural College, Cirencester. With 68 Illustrations. 1s. 6d.

240. *IRRIGATION AND WATER SUPPLY.* A Treatise on Water Meadows, Sewage Irrigation, and Warping; the Construction of Wells, Ponds, and Reservoirs, &c. By Prof. JOHN SCOTT. With 34 Illus. 1s. 6d.

241. *FARM ROADS, FENCES, AND GATES.* A Practical Treatise on the Roads, Tramways, and Waterways of the Farm; the Principles of Enclosures; and the different kinds of Fences, Gates, and Stiles. By Professor JOHN SCOTT. With 75 Illustrations. 1s. 6d.

242. *FARM BUILDINGS.* A Practical Treatise on the Buildings necessary for various kinds of Farms, their Arrangement and Construction, with Plans and Estimates. By Prof. JOHN SCOTT. With 105 Illus. 2s.

243. *BARN IMPLEMENTS AND MACHINES.* A Practical Treatise on the Application of Power to the Operations of Agriculture; and on various Machines used in the Threshing-barn, in the Stock-yard, and in the Dairy, &c. By Prof. J. SCOTT. With 123 Illustrations. 2s.

244. *FIELD IMPLEMENTS AND MACHINES.* A Practical Treatise on the Varieties now in use, with Principles and Details of Construction, their Points of Excellence, and Management. By Professor JOHN SCOTT. With 138 Illustrations. 2s.

245. *AGRICULTURAL SURVEYING.* A Practical Treatise on Land Surveying, Levelling, and Setting-out; and on Measuring and Estimating Quantities, Weights, and Values of Materials, Produce, Stock, &c. By Prof. JOHN SCOTT. With 62 Illustrations. 1s. 6d.

⁂ *Nos. 239 to 245 in One Vol., handsomely half-bound, entitled* "THE COMPLETE TEXT-BOOK OF FARM ENGINEERING." By Professor JOHN SCOTT. *Price 12s.*

250. *MEAT PRODUCTION.* A Manual for Producers, Distributors, &c. By JOHN EWART. 2s. 6d.‡

266. *BOOK-KEEPING FOR FARMERS & ESTATE OWNERS.* By J. M. WOODMAN, Chartered Accountant. 2s. 6d. cloth limp; 3s. 6d. cloth boards.　　　　　　　　　　　*[Just published.*

☞ *The ‡ indicates that these vols. may be had strongly bound at 6d. extra.*

LONDON : CROSBY LOCKWOOD AND SON,

MATHEMATICS, ARITHMETIC, ETC.

32. *MATHEMATICAL INSTRUMENTS*, a Treatise on; Their Construction, Adjustment, Testing, and Use concisely Explained. By J. F. HEATHER, M.A. Fourteenth Edition, revised, with additions, by A. T. WALMISLEY, M.I.C.E., Fellow of the Surveyors' Institution. Original Edition, in 1 vol., Illustrated. 2s.‡ [*Just published.*]

** *In ordering the above, be careful to say, " Original Edition " (No. 32), to distinguish it from the Enlarged Edition in 3 vols. (Nos. 168-9-70.)*

76. *DESCRIPTIVE GEOMETRY*, an Elementary Treatise on; with a Theory of Shadows and of Perspective, extracted from the French of G. MONGE. To which is added, a description of the Principles and Practice of Isometrical Projection. By J. F. HEATHER, M.A. With 14 Plates. 2s.

178. *PRACTICAL PLANE GEOMETRY:* giving the Simplest Modes of Constructing Figures contained in one Plane and Geometrical Construction of the Ground. By J. F. HEATHER, M.A. With 215 Woodcuts. 2s.

83. *COMMERCIAL BOOK-KEEPING.* With Commercial Phrases and Forms in English, French, Italian, and German. By JAMES HADDON, M.A., Arithmetical Master of King's College School, London. 1s. 6d.

84. *ARITHMETIC*, a Rudimentary Treatise on: with full Explanations of its Theoretical Principles, and numerous Examples for Practice. By Professor J. R. YOUNG. Eleventh Edition. 1s. 6d.

84*. A KEY to the above, containing Solutions in full to the Exercises, together with Comments, Explanations, and Improved Processes, for the Use of Teachers and Unassisted Learners. By J. R. YOUNG. 1s. 6d.

85. *EQUATIONAL ARITHMETIC*, applied to Questions of Interest, Annuities, Life Assurance, and General Commerce; with various Tables by which all Calculations may be greatly facilitated. By W. HIPSLEY. 2s.

86. *ALGEBRA*, the Elements of. By JAMES HADDON, M.A. With Appendix, containing miscellaneous Investigations, and a Collection of Problems in various parts of Algebra. 2s.

86*. A KEY AND COMPANION to the above Book, forming an extensive repository of Solved Examples and Problems in Illustration of the various Expedients necessary in Algebraical Operations. By J. R. YOUNG. 1s. 6d.

88. *EUCLID*, THE ELEMENTS OF: with many additional Propositions
89. and Explanatory Notes: to which is prefixed, an Introductory Essay on Logic. By HENRY LAW, C.E. 2s. 6d.‡

** *Sold also separately, viz. :—*

88. EUCLID, The First Three Books. By HENRY LAW, C.E. 1s. 6d.
89. EUCLID, Books 4, 5, 6, 11, 12. By HENRY LAW, C.E. 1s. 6d.

90. *ANALYTICAL GEOMETRY AND CONIC SECTIONS*, By JAMES HANN. A New Edition, by Professor J. R. YOUNG. 2s.‡

91. *PLANE TRIGONOMETRY*, the Elements of. By JAMES HANN, formerly Mathematical Master of King's College, London. 1s. 6d.

92. *SPHERICAL TRIGONOMETRY*, the Elements of. By JAMES HANN. Revised by CHARLES H. DOWLING, C.E. 1s.
** *Or with " The Elements of Plane Trigonometry," in One Volume,* 2s. 6d.

93. *MENSURATION AND MEASURING.* With the Mensuration and Levelling of Land for the Purposes of Modern Engineering. By T. BAKER, C.E. New Edition by E. NUGENT, C.E. Illustrated. 1s. 6d.

101. *DIFFERENTIAL CALCULUS*, Elements of the. By W. S. B. WOOLHOUSE, F.R.A.S., &c. 1s. 6d.

102. *INTEGRAL CALCULUS*, Rudimentary Treatise on the. By HOMERSHAM COX, B.A. Illustrated. 1s.

136. *ARITHMETIC*, Rudimentary, for the Use of Schools and Self-Instruction. By JAMES HADDON, M.A. Revised by A. ARMAN. 1s. 6d.
137. A KEY TO HADDON'S RUDIMENTARY ARITHMETIC. By A. ARMAN. 1s. 6d.

☞ *The ‡ indicates that these vols. may be had strongly bound at 6d. extra.*

7, STATIONERS' HALL COURT, LUDGATE HILL, E.C.

Mathematics, Arithmetic, etc., *continued*.

168. *DRAWING AND MEASURING INSTRUMENTS.* Including—I. Instruments employed in Geometrical and Mechanical Drawing, and in the Construction, Copying, and Measurement of Maps and Plans. II. Instruments used for the purposes of Accurate Measurement, and for Arithmetical Computations. By J. F. HEATHER, M.A. Illustrated. 1s. 6d.

169. *OPTICAL INSTRUMENTS.* Including (more especially) Telescopes, Microscopes, and Apparatus for producing copies of Maps and Plans by Photography. By J. F. HEATHER, M.A. Illustrated. 1s. 6d.

170. *SURVEYING AND ASTRONOMICAL INSTRUMENTS.* Including—I. Instruments Used for Determining the Geometrical Features of a portion of Ground. II. Instruments Employed in Astronomical Observations. By J. F. HEATHER, M.A. Illustrated. 1s. 6d.

⁎ *The above three volumes form an enlargement of the Author's original work "Mathematical Instruments." (See No. 32 in the Series.)*

168.)
169.} *MATHEMATICAL INSTRUMENTS.* By J. F. HEATHER, M.A. Enlarged Edition, for the most part entirely re-written. The 3 Parts as
170.) above, in One thick Volume. With numerous Illustrations. 4s. 6d.‡

158. *THE SLIDE RULE, AND HOW TO USE IT;* containing full, easy, and simple Instructions to perform all Business Calculations with unexampled rapidity and accuracy. By CHARLES HOARE, C.E. Fifth Edition. With a Slide Rule in tuck of cover. 2s. 6d.‡

196. *THEORY OF COMPOUND INTEREST AND ANNUI-TIES;* with Tables of Logarithms for the more Difficult Computations of Interest, Discount, Annuities, &c. By FÉDOR THOMAN. 4s.‡

199. *THE COMPENDIOUS CALCULATOR;* or, Easy and Concise Methods of Performing the various Arithmetical Operations required in Commercial and Business Transactions; together with Useful Tables. By D. O'GORMAN. Twenty-seventh Edition, carefully revised by C. NORRIS. 2s. 6d., cloth limp; 3s. 6d., strongly half-bound in leather.

204. *MATHEMATICAL TABLES,* for Trigonometrical, Astronomical, and Nautical Calculations; to which is prefixed a Treatise on Logarithms. By HENRY LAW, C.E. Together with a Series of Tables for Navigation and Nautical Astronomy. By Prof. J. R. YOUNG. New Edition. 4s.

204⁎. *LOGARITHMS.* With Mathematical Tables for Trigonometrical, Astronomical, and Nautical Calculations. By HENRY LAW, M.Inst.C.E. New and Revised Edition. (Forming part of the above Work). 3s.

221. *MEASURES, WEIGHTS, AND MONEYS OF ALL NA-TIONS,* and an Analysis of the Christian, Hebrew, and Mahometan Calendars. By W. S. B. WOOLHOUSE, F.R.A.S., F.S.S. Sixth Edition. 2s.‡

227. *MATHEMATICS AS APPLIED TO THE CONSTRUC-TIVE ARTS.* Illustrating the various processes of Mathematical Investigation, by means of Arithmetical and Simple Algebraical Equations and Practical Examples. By FRANCIS CAMPIN. C.E. Second Edition. 3s.‡

PHYSICAL SCIENCE, NATURAL PHILO-SOPHY, ETC.

1. *CHEMISTRY.* By Professor GEORGE FOWNES, F.R.S. With an Appendix on the Application of Chemistry to Agriculture. 1s.

2. *NATURAL PHILOSOPHY,* Introduction to the Study of. By C. TOMLINSON. Woodcuts. 1s. 6d.

6. *MECHANICS,* Rudimentary Treatise on. By CHARLES TOMLINSON. Illustrated. 1s. 6d.

7. *ELECTRICITY;* showing the General Principles of Electrical Science, and the purposes to which it has been applied. By Sir W. SNOW HARRIS, F.R.S., &c. With Additions by R. SABINE, C.E., F.S.A. 1s. 6d.

7⁎. *GALVANISM.* By Sir W. SNOW HARRIS. New Edition by ROBERT SABINE, C.E., F.S.A. 1s. 6d.

8. *MAGNETISM;* being a concise Exposition of the General Principles of Magnetical Science. By Sir W. SNOW HARRIS. New Edition, revised by H. M. NOAD, Ph.D. With 165 Woodcuts. 3s. 6d.‡

☞ *The ‡ indicates that these vols. may be had strongly bound at 6d. extra.*

Physical Science, Natural Philosophy, etc., *continued.*

11. *THE ELECTRIC TELEGRAPH;* its History and Progress; with Descriptions of some of the Apparatus. By R. SABINE, C.E., F.S.A. 3s.

12. *PNEUMATICS,* including Acoustics and the Phenomena of Wind Currents, for the Use of Beginners By CHARLES TOMLINSON, F.R.S. Fourth Edition, enlarged. Illustrated. 1s. 6d. [*Just published.*]

72. *MANUAL OF THE MOLLUSCA;* a Treatise on Recent and Fossil Shells. By Dr. S. P. WOODWARD, A.L.S. Fourth Edition. With Appendix by RALPH TATE, A.L.S., F.G.S. With numerous Plates and 300 Woodcuts. 6s. 6d. Cloth boards, 7s. 6d.

96. *ASTRONOMY.* By the late Rev. ROBERT MAIN, M.A. Third Edition, by WILLIAM THYNNE LYNN, B.A., F.R.A.S. 2s.

97. *STATICS AND DYNAMICS,* the Principles and Practice of; embracing also a clear development of Hydrostatics, Hydrodynamics, and Central Forces. By T. BAKER, C.E. Fourth Edition. 1s. 6d.

138. *TELEGRAPH,* Handbook of the; a Guide to Candidates for Employment in the Telegraph Service. By R. BOND. 3s.‡

173. *PHYSICAL GEOLOGY,* partly based on Major-General PORT-LOCK's "Rudiments of Geology." By RALPH TATE, A.L.S., &c. Woodcuts. 2s.

174. *HISTORICAL GEOLOGY,* partly based on Major-General PORTLOCK's "Rudiments." By RALPH TATE, A.L.S., &c. Woodcuts. 2s. 6d.

173 & 174. *RUDIMENTARY TREATISE ON GEOLOGY,* Physical and Historical. Partly based on Major-General PORTLOCK's "Rudiments of Geology." By RALPH TATE, A.L.S., F.G.S., &c. In One Volume. 4s. 6d.‡

183 & 184. *ANIMAL PHYSICS,* Handbook of. By Dr. LARDNER, D.C.L., formerly Professor of Natural Philosophy and Astronomy in University College, Lond. With 520 Illustrations. In One Vol. 7s. 6d., cloth boards.
*** *Sold also in Two Parts, as follows:—*

183. ANIMAL PHYSICS. By Dr. LARDNER. Part I., Chapters I.—VII. 4s.

184. ANIMAL PHYSICS. By Dr. LARDNER. Part II., Chapters VIII.—XVIII. 3s.

FINE ARTS.

20. *PERSPECTIVE FOR BEGINNERS.* Adapted to Young Students and Amateurs in Architecture, Painting, &c. By GEORGE PYNE. 2s.

40 *GLASS STAINING, AND THE ART OF PAINTING ON GLASS.* From the German of Dr. GESSERT and EMANUEL OTTO FROMBERG. With an Appendix on THE ART OF ENAMELLING. 2s. 6d.

69. *MUSIC,* A Rudimentary and Practical Treatise on. With numerous Examples. By CHARLES CHILD SPENCER. 2s. 6d.

71. *PIANOFORTE,* The Art of Playing the. With numerous Exercises & Lessons from the Best Masters. By CHARLES CHILD SPENCER. 1s.6d.

69-71. *MUSIC & THE PIANOFORTE.* In one vol. Half bound, 5s.

181. *PAINTING POPULARLY EXPLAINED,* including Fresco, Oil, Mosaic, Water Colour, Water-Glass, Tempera, Encaustic, Miniature, Painting on Ivory, Vellum, Pottery, Enamel, Glass, &c. With Historical Sketches of the Progress of the Art by THOMAS JOHN GULLICK, assisted by JOHN TIMBS, F.S.A. Fifth Edition, revised and enlarged. 5s.‡

186. *A GRAMMAR OF COLOURING,* applied to Decorative Painting and the Arts. By GEORGE FIELD. New Edition, enlarged and adapted to the Use of the Ornamental Painter and Designer. By ELLIS A. DAVIDSON. With two new Coloured Diagrams, &c. 3s.‡

246. *A DICTIONARY OF PAINTERS, AND HANDBOOK FOR PICTURE AMATEURS;* including Methods of Painting, Cleaning, Re-lining and Restoring, Schools of Painting, &c. With Notes on the Copyists and Imitators of each Master. By PHILIPPE DARYL. 2s. 6d.‡

The ‡ indicates that these vols. may be had strongly bound at 6d. extra.

7, STATIONERS' HALL COURT, LUDGATE HILL, E.C.

INDUSTRIAL AND USEFUL ARTS.

23. *BRICKS AND TILES*, Rudimentary Treatise on the Manufacture of. By E. Dobson, M.R.I.B.A. Illustrated, 3s.‡

67. *CLOCKS, WATCHES, AND BELLS*, a Rudimentary Treatise on. By Sir Edmund Beckett, LL.D., Q.C. Seventh Edition, revised and enlarged. 4s. 6d. limp; 5s. 6d. cloth boards.

83**. *CONSTRUCTION OF DOOR LOCKS.* Compiled from the Papers of A. C. Hobbs, and Edited by Charles Tomlinson. F.R.S. 2s. 6d.

162. *THE BRASS FOUNDER'S MANUAL;* Instructions for Modelling, Pattern-Making, Moulding, Turning, Filing, Burnishing, Bronzing, &c. With copious Receipts, &c. By Walter Graham. 2s.‡

205. *THE ART OF LETTER PAINTING MADE EASY.* By J. G. Badenoch. Illustrated with 12 full-page Engravings of Examples. 1s. 6d.

215. *THE GOLDSMITH'S HANDBOOK,* containing full Instructions for the Alloying and Working of Gold. By George E. Gee, 3s.‡

225. *THE SILVERSMITH'S HANDBOOK,* containing full Instructions for the Alloying and Working of Silver. By George E. Gee. 3s.‡

₊ *The two preceding Works, in One handsome Vol., half-bound, entitled "The Goldsmith's & Silversmith's Complete Handbook," 7s.*

249. *THE HALL-MARKING OF JEWELLERY PRACTICALLY CONSIDERED.* By George E. Gee. 3s.‡

224. *COACH BUILDING*, A Practical Treatise, Historical and Descriptive. By J. W. Burgess. 2s. 6d.‡

235. *PRACTICAL ORGAN BUILDING.* By W. E. Dickson, M.A., Precentor of Ely Cathedral. Illustrated. 2s. 6d.‡

262. *THE ART OF BOOT AND SHOEMAKING*, including Measurement, 'Last-fitting, Cutting-out, Closing and Making. By John Bedford Leno. Numerous Illustrations. Third Edition. 2s.

263. *MECHANICAL DENTISTRY:* A Practical Treatise on the Construction of the Various Kinds of Artificial Dentures, with Formulæ, Tables, Receipts, &c. By Charles Hunter. Third Edition. 3s.‡

MISCELLANEOUS VOLUMES.

36. *A DICTIONARY OF TERMS used in ARCHITECTURE, BUILDING, ENGINEERING, MINING, METALLURGY, ARCHÆOLOGY, the FINE ARTS, &c.* By John Weale. Fifth Edition. Revised by Robert Hunt, F.R.S. Illustrated. 5s. limp; 6s. cloth boards.

50. *THE LAW OF CONTRACTS FOR WORKS AND SERVICES.* By David Gibbons. Third Edition, enlarged. 3s.‡

112. *MANUAL OF DOMESTIC MEDICINE.* By R. Gooding, B.A., M.D. A Family Guide in all Cases of Accident and Emergency. 2s.‡

112*. *MANAGEMENT OF HEALTH.* A Manual of Home and Personal Hygiene. By the Rev. James Baird, B.A. 1s.

150. *LOGIC*, Pure and Applied. By S. H. Emmens. 1s. 6d.

153. *SELECTIONS FROM LOCKE'S ESSAYS ON THE HUMAN UNDERSTANDING.* With Notes by S. H. Emmens. 2s.

154. *GENERAL HINTS TO EMIGRANTS.* 2s.

157. *THE EMIGRANT'S GUIDE TO NATAL.* By Robert James Mann, F.R.A.S., F.M.S. Second Edition. Map. 2s.

193. *HANDBOOK OF FIELD FORTIFICATION.* By Major W. W. Knollys, F.R.G.S. With 163 Woodcuts. 3s.‡

194. *THE HOUSE MANAGER:* Being a Guide to Housekeeping. Practical Cookery, Pickling and Preserving, Household Work, Dairy Management, &c. By An Old Housekeeper. 3s. 6d.‡

194, *HOUSE BOOK (The).* Comprising:—I. The House Manager.
112 & By an Old Housekeeper. II. Domestic Medicine. By R. Gooding, M.D.
112*. III. Management of Health. By J. Baird. In One Vol., half-bound, 6s.

☞ *The ‡ indicates that these vols. may be had strongly bound at 6d. extra.*

LONDON : CROSBY LOCKWOOD AND SON,

EDUCATIONAL AND CLASSICAL SERIES.

HISTORY.

1. **England, Outlines of the History of;** more especially with reference to the Origin and Progress of the English Constitution. By WILLIAM DOUGLAS HAMILTON, F.S.A., of Her Majesty's Public Record Office. 4th Edition, revised. 5s.; cloth boards, 6s.

5. **Greece, Outlines of the History of;** in connection with the Rise of the Arts and Civilization in Europe. By W. DOUGLAS HAMILTON, of University College, London, and EDWARD LEVIEN, M.A., of Balliol College, Oxford. 2s. 6d.; cloth boards, 3s. 6d.

7. **Rome, Outlines of the History of:** from the Earliest Period to the Christian Era and the Commencement of the Decline of the Empire. By EDWARD LEVIEN, of Balliol College, Oxford. Map, 2s. 6d.; cl. bds. 3s. 6d.

9. **Chronology of History, Art, Literature, and Progress,** from the Creation of the World to the Present Time. The Continuation by W. D. HAMILTON, F.S.A. 3s.; cloth boards, 3s. 6d.

50. **Dates and Events in English History,** for the use of Candidates in Public and Private Examinations. By the Rev. E. RAND. 1s.

ENGLISH LANGUAGE AND MISCELLANEOUS.

11. **Grammar of the English Tongue,** Spoken and Written. With an Introduction to the Study of Comparative Philology. By HYDE CLARKE, D.C.L. Fourth Edition. 1s. 6d.

11*. **Philology :** Handbook of the Comparative Philology of English, Anglo-Saxon, Frisian, Flemish or Dutch, Low or Platt Dutch, High Dutch or German, Danish, Swedish, Icelandic, Latin, Italian, French, Spanish, and Portuguese Tongues. By HYDE CLARKE, D.C.L. 1s.

12. **Dictionary of the English Language,** as Spoken and Written. Containing above 100,000 Words. By HYDE CLARKE, D.C.L. 3s. 6d.; cloth boards, 4s. 6d.; complete with the GRAMMAR, cloth bds., 5s. 6d.

48. **Composition and Punctuation,** familiarly Explained for those who have neglected the Study of Grammar. By JUSTIN BRENAN. 18th Edition. 1s. 6d.

49. **Derivative Spelling-Book :** Giving the Origin of Every Word from the Greek, Latin, Saxon, German, Teutonic, Dutch, French, Spanish, and other Languages; with their present Acceptation and Pronunciation. By J. ROWBOTHAM, F.R.A.S. Improved Edition. 1s. 6d.

51. **The Art of Extempore Speaking :** Hints for the Pulpit, the Senate, and the Bar. By M. BAUTAIN, Vicar-General and Professor at the Sorbonne. Translated from the French. 8th Edition, carefully corrected. 2s. 6d.

53. **Places and Facts in Political and Physical Geography,** for Candidates in Examinations. By the Rev. EDGAR RAND, B.A. 1s.

54. **Analytical Chemistry, Qualitative and Quantitative, a Course** of. To which is prefixed, a Brief Treatise upon Modern Chemical Nomenclature and Notation. By WM. W. PINK and GEORGE E. WEBSTER. 2s.

THE SCHOOL MANAGERS' SERIES OF READING BOOKS,

Edited by the Rev. A. R. GRANT, Rector of Hitcham, and Honorary Canon of Ely; formerly H.M. Inspector of Schools.
INTRODUCTORY PRIMER, 3d.

	s.	d.					s.	d.
FIRST STANDARD	. 0	6	FOURTH STANDARD	.	.	.	1	2
SECOND ,,	. 0	10	FIFTH ,,	.	.	.	1	6
THIRD ,,	. 1	0	SIXTH ,,	.	.	.	1	6

LESSONS FROM THE BIBLE. Part I. Old Testament. 1s.
LESSONS FROM THE BIBLE. Part II. New Testament, to which is added THE GEOGRAPHY OF THE BIBLE, for very young Children. By Rev. C. THORNTON FORSTER. 1s. 2d. *.* Or the Two Parts in One Volume. 2s.

FRENCH.

24. **French Grammar.** With Complete and Concise Rules on the Genders of French Nouns. By G. L. STRAUSS, Ph.D. 1s. 6d.
25. **French-English Dictionary.** Comprising a large number of New Terms used in Engineering, Mining, &c. By ALFRED ELWES. 1s. 6d.
26. **English-French Dictionary.** By ALFRED ELWES. 2s.
25,26. **French Dictionary** (as above). Complete, in One Vol., 3s.; cloth boards, 3s. 6d. *.* Or with the GRAMMAR, cloth boards, 4s. 6d.
47. **French and English Phrase Book :** containing Introductory Lessons, with Translations, several Vocabularies of Words, a Collection of suitable Phrases, and Easy Familiar Dialogues. 1s. 6d.

GERMAN.

39. **German Grammar.** Adapted for English Students, from Heyse's Theoretical and Practical Grammar, by Dr. G. L. STRAUSS. 1s. 6d.
40. **German Reader :** A Series of Extracts, carefully culled from the most approved Authors of Germany; with Notes, Philological and Explanatory. By G. L. STRAUSS, Ph.D. 1s.
41-43. **German Triglot Dictionary.** By N. E. S. A. HAMILTON. In Three Parts. Part I. German-French-English. Part II. English-German-French. Part III. French-German-English. 3s., or cloth boards, 4s.
41-43 & 39. **German Triglot Dictionary** (as above), together with German Grammar (No. 39), in One Volume, cloth boards, 5s.

ITALIAN.

27. **Italian Grammar,** arranged in Twenty Lessons, with a Course of Exercises. By ALFRED ELWES. 1s. 6d.
28. **Italian Triglot Dictionary,** wherein the Genders of all the Italian and French Nouns are carefully noted down. By ALFRED ELWES. Vol. 1. Italian-English-French. 2s. 6d.
30. **Italian Triglot Dictionary.** By A. ELWES. Vol. 2. English-French-Italian. 2s. 6d.
32. **Italian Triglot Dictionary.** By ALFRED ELWES. Vol. 3. French-Italian-English. 2s. 6d.
28,30, **Italian Triglot Dictionary** (as above). In One Vol., 7s. 6d. 32. Cloth boards.

SPANISH AND PORTUGUESE.

34. **Spanish Grammar,** in a Simple and Practical Form. With a Course of Exercises. By ALFRED ELWES. 1s. 6d.
35. **Spanish-English and English-Spanish Dictionary.** Including a large number of Technical Terms used in Mining, Engineering, &c. with the proper Accents and the Gender of every Noun. By ALFRED ELWES 4s.; cloth boards, 5s. *.* Or with the GRAMMAR, cloth boards, 6s.
55. **Portuguese Grammar,** in a Simple and Practical Form. With a Course of Exercises. By ALFRED ELWES. 1s. 6d.
56. **Portuguese-English and English-Portuguese Dictionary.** Including a large number of Technical Terms used in Mining, Engineering, &c., with the proper Accents and the Gender of every Noun. By ALFRED ELWES. Second Edition, Revised, 5s.; cloth boards, 6s. *.* Or with the GRAMMAR, cloth boards, 7s.

HEBREW.

46*. **Hebrew Grammar.** By Dr. BRESSLAU. 1s. 6d.
44. **Hebrew and English Dictionary,** Biblical and Rabbinical; containing the Hebrew and Chaldee Roots of the Old Testament Post-Rabbinical Writings. By Dr. BRESSLAU. 6s.
46. **English and Hebrew Dictionary.** By Dr. BRESSLAU. 3s.
44,46. **Hebrew Dictionary** (as above), in Two Vols., complete, with 46*. the GRAMMAR, cloth boards, 12s.

LATIN.

19. **Latin Grammar.** Containing the Inflections and Elementary Principles of Translation and Construction. By the Rev. THOMAS GOODWIN, M.A., Head Master of the Greenwich Proprietary School. 1s. 6d.

20. **Latin-English Dictionary.** By the Rev. THOMAS GOODWIN, M.A. 2s.

22. **English-Latin Dictionary;** together with an Appendix of French and Italian Words which have their origin from the Latin. By the Rev. THOMAS GOODWIN, M.A. 1s. 6d.

20,22. **Latin Dictionary** (as above). Complete in One Vol., 3s. 6d. cloth boards, 4s. 6d. •.• Or with the GRAMMAR, cloth boards, 5s. 6d.

LATIN CLASSICS. With Explanatory Notes in English.

1. **Latin Delectus.** Containing Extracts from Classical Authors, with Genealogical Vocabularies and Explanatory Notes, by H. YOUNG. 1s. 6d;

2. **Cæsaris Commentarii de Bello Gallico.** Notes, and a Geographical Register for the Use of Schools, by H. YOUNG. 2s.

3. **Cornelius Nepos.** With Notes. By H. YOUNG. 1s.

4. **Virgilii** Maronis Bucolica et Georgica. With Notes on the Bucolics by W. RUSHTON, M.A., and on the Georgics by H. YOUNG. 1s. 6d.

5. **Virgilii** Maronis Æneis. With Notes, Critical and Explanatory, by H. YOUNG. New Edition, revised and improved. With copious Additional Notes by Rev. T. H. L. LEARY, D.C.L., formerly Scholar of Brasenose College, Oxford. 3s.

5*. —— Part 1. Books i.—vi., 1s. 6d.

5**. —— Part 2. Books vii.—xii., 2s.

6. **Horace;** Odes, Epode, and Carmen Sæculare. Notes by H. YOUNG. 1s. 6d.

7. **Horace;** Satires, Epistles, and Ars Poetica. Notes by W. BROWNRIGG SMITH, M.A., F.R.G.S. 1s. 6d.

8. **Sallustii Crispi Catalina et Bellum Jugurthinum.** Notes, Critical and Explanatory, by W. M. DONNE, B.A., Trin. Coll., Cam. 1s. 6d.

9. **Terentii Andria et Heautontimorumenos.** With Notes, Critical and Explanatory, by the Rev. JAMES DAVIES, M.A. 1s. 6d.

10. **Terentii Adelphi, Hecyra, Phormio.** Edited, with Notes, Critical and Explanatory, by the Rev. JAMES DAVIES, M.A. 2s.

11. **Terentii Eunuchus, Comœdia.** Notes, by Rev. J. DAVIES, M.A. 1s. 6d.

12. **Ciceronis Oratio pro Sexto Roscio Amerino.** Edited, with an Introduction, Analysis, and Notes, Explanatory and Critical, by the Rev. JAMES DAVIES, M.A. 1s. 6d.

13. **Ciceronis Orationes in Catilinam, Verrem, et pro Archia.** With Introduction, Analysis, and Notes, Explanatory and Critical, by Rev. T. H. L. LEARY, D.C.L. formerly Scholar of Brasenose College, Oxford. 1s. 6d.

14. **Ciceronis Cato Major, Lælius, Brutus, sive de Senectute, de Amicitia, de Claris Oratoribus Dialogi.** With Notes by W. BROWNRIGG SMITH, M.A., F.R.G.S. 2s.

16. **Livy:** History of Rome. Notes by H. YOUNG and W. B. SMITH, M.A. Part 1. Books i., ii., 1s. 6d.

16*. —— Part 2. Books iii., iv., v., 1s. 6d.

17. —— Part 3. Books xxi., xxii., 1s. 6d.

19. **Latin Verse Selections,** from Catullus, Tibullus, Propertius, and Ovid. Notes by W. B. DONNE, M.A., Trinity College, Cambridge. 2s.

20. **Latin Prose Selections,** from Varro, Columella, Vitruvius, Seneca, Quintilian, Florus, Velleius Paterculus, Valerius Maximus Suetonius, Apuleius, &c. Notes by W. B. DONNE, M.A. 2s.

21. **Juvenalis Satiræ.** With Prolegomena and Notes by T. H. S. ESCOTT, B.A., Lecturer on Logic at King's College, London. 2s.

GREEK.

14. **Greek Grammar,** in accordance with the Principles and Philological Researches of the most eminent Scholars of our own day. By HANS CLAUDE HAMILTON. 1s. 6d.

15,17. **Greek Lexicon.** Containing all the Words in General Use, with their Significations, Inflections, and Doubtful Quantities. By HENRY R. HAMILTON. Vol. 1. Greek-English, 2s. 6d.; Vol. 2. English-Greek, 2s. Or the Two Vols. in One, 4s. 6d.: cloth boards, 5s.

14,15. **Greek Lexicon** (as above). Complete, with the GRAMMAR, in
17.   One Vol., cloth boards, 6s.

GREEK CLASSICS. With Explanatory Notes in English.

1. **Greek Delectus.** Containing Extracts from Classical Authors, with Genealogical Vocabularies and Explanatory Notes, by H. YOUNG. New Edition, with an improved and enlarged Supplementary Vocabulary, by JOHN HUTCHISON, M.A., of the High School, Glasgow. 1s. 6d.

2, 3. **Xenophon's Anabasis;** or, The Retreat of the Ten Thousand. Notes and a Geographical Register, by H. YOUNG. Part 1. Books i. to iii., 1s. Part 2. Books iv. to vii., 1s.

4. **Lucian's Select Dialogues.** The Text carefully revised, with Grammatical and Explanatory Notes, by H. YOUNG. 1s. 6d.

5-12. **Homer, The Works of.** According to the Text of BAEUMLEIN. With Notes, Critical and Explanatory, drawn from the best and latest Authorities, with Preliminary Observations and Appendices, by T. H. L. LEARY, M.A., D.C.L.

THE ILIAD:	Part 1. Books i. to vi., 1s. 6d.	Part 3. Books xiii. to xviii., 1s. 6d.
	Part 2. Books vii. to xii., 1s. 6d.	Part 4. Books xix. to xxiv., 1s. 6d.
THE ODYSSEY:	Part 1. Books i. to vi., 1s. 6d	Part 3. Books xiii. to xviii., 1s. 6d.
	Part 2. Books vii. to xii., 1s. 6d.	Part 4. Books xix. to xxiv., and Hymns, 2s.

13. **Plato's Dialogues:** The Apology of Socrates, the Crito, and the Phædo. From the Text of C. F. HERMANN. Edited with Notes, Critical and Explanatory, by the Rev. JAMES DAVIES, M.A. 2s.

14-17. **Herodotus, The History of,** chiefly after the Text of GAISFORD. With Preliminary Observations and Appendices, and Notes, Critical and Explanatory, by T. H. L. LEARY, M.A., D.C.L.
    Part 1.   Books i., ii. (The Clio and Euterpe), 2s.
    Part 2.   Books iii., iv. (The Thalia and Melpomene), 2s.
    Part 3.   Books v.-vii. (The Terpsichore, Erato, and Polymnia), 2s.
    Part 4.   Books viii., ix. (The Urania and Calliope) and Index, 1s. 6d.

18. **Sophocles: Œdipus Tyrannus.** Notes by H. YOUNG. 1s.

20. **Sophocles: Antigone.** From the Text of DINDORF. Notes, Critical and Explanatory, by the Rev. JOHN MILNER, B.A. 2s.

23. **Euripides: Hecuba and Medea.** Chiefly from the Text of DINDORF. With Notes, Critical and Explanatory, by W. BROWNRIGG SMITH, M.A., F.R.G.S. 1s. 6d.

26. **Euripides: Alcestis.** Chiefly from the Text of DINDORF. With Notes, Critical and Explanatory, by JOHN MILNER, B.A. 1s. 6d.

30. **Æschylus: Prometheus Vinctus:** The Prometheus Bound. From the Text of DINDORF. Edited, with English Notes, Critical and Explanatory, by the Rev. JAMES DAVIES, M.A. 1s.

32. **Æschylus: Septem Contra Thebes:** The Seven against Thebes. From the Text of DINDORF. Edited, with English Notes, Critical and Explanatory, by the Rev. JAMES DAVIES, M.A. 1s.

40. **Aristophanes: Acharnians.** Chiefly from the Text of C. H. WEISE. With Notes, by C. S. T. TOWNSHEND, M.A. 1s. 6d.

41. **Thucydides:** History of the Peloponnesian War. Notes by H. YOUNG. Book 1. 1s. 6d.

42. **Xenophon's Panegyric on Agesilaus.** Notes and Introduction by LL. F. W. JEWITT. 1s. 6d.

43. **Demosthenes.** The Oration on the Crown and the Philippics. With English Notes. By Rev. T. H. L. LEARY, D.C.L., formerly Scholar of Brasenose College, Oxford. 1s. 6d.

7, STATIONERS' HALL COURT, LONDON, E.C,
October 1889.

A

CATALOGUE OF BOOKS

INCLUDING MANY NEW AND STANDARD WORKS IN

ENGINEERING, MECHANICS, ARCHITECTURE,

NATURAL AND APPLIED SCIENCE,

INDUSTRIAL ARTS, TRADE AND COMMERCE, AGRICULTURE,

GARDENING, LAND MANAGEMENT, LAW, &c.

PUBLISHED BY

CROSBY LOCKWOOD & SON.

MECHANICS, MECHANICAL ENGINEERING, etc

New Manual for Practical Engineers.

THE PRACTICAL ENGINEER'S HAND-BOOK. Comprising a Treatise on Modern Engines and Boilers: Marine, Locomotive and Stationary. And containing a large collection of Rules and Practical Data relating to recent Practice in Designing and Constructing all kinds of Engines, Boilers, and other Engineering work. The whole constituting a comprehensive Key to the Board of Trade and other Examinations for Certificates of Competency in Modern Mechanical Engineering. By WALTER S. HUTTON, Civil and Mechanical Engineer, Author of "The Works' Manager's Handbook for Engineers," &c. With upwards of 370 Illustrations. Third Edition, Revised, with Additions. Medium 8vo, nearly 500 pp., price 18s. Strongly bound. *[Just published.*

☞ *This work is designed as a companion to the Author's "*WORKS' MANAGER'S HAND-BOOK.*" It possesses many new and original features, and contains, like its predecessor, a quantity of matter not originally intended for publication, but collected by the author for his own use in the construction of a great variety of modern engineering work.*

The information is given in a condensed and concise form, and is illustrated by upwards of 370 Woodcuts ; and comprises a quantity of tabulated matter of great value to all engaged in designing, constructing, or estimating for ENGINES, BOILERS *and* OTHER ENGINEERING WORK.

*** OPINIONS OF THE PRESS.

" We have kept it at hand for several weeks, referring to it as occasion arose, and we have not n a single occasion consulted its pages without finding the information of which we were in quest." *Athenæum.*

" A thoroughly good practical handbook, which no engineer can go through without learning something that will be of service to him."—*Marine Engineer.*

" An excellent book of reference for engineers, and a valuable text-book for students of engineering."—*Scotsman.*

" This valuable manual embodies the results and experience of the leading authorities on mechanical engineering."—*Building News.*

" The author has collected together a surprising quantity of rules and practical data, and has shown much judgment in the selections he has made. . . . There is no doubt that this book is one of the most useful of its kind published, and will be a very popular compendium."—*Engineer.*

" A mass of information, set down in simple language, and in such a form that it can be easily referred to at any time. The matter is uniformly good and well chosen, and is greatly elucidated by the illustrations. The book will find its way on to most engineers' shelves, where it will rank as one of the most useful books of reference."—*Practical Engineer.*

" Full of useful information, and should be found on the office shelf of all practical engineers." —*English Mechanic.*

Handbook for Works' Managers.

THE WORKS' MANAGER'S HANDBOOK OF MODERN RULES, TABLES, AND DATA. For Engineers, Millwrights, and Boiler Makers; Tool Makers, Machinists, and Metal Workers; Iron and Brass Founders, &c. By W. S. HUTTON, Civil and Mechanical Engineer, Author of "The Practical Engineer's Handbook." Third Edition, carefully Revised, with Additions. In One handsome Vol., medium 8vo price 15s. strongly bound.

☞ *The Author having compiled Rules and Data for his own use in a great variety of modern engineering work, and having found his notes extremely useful, decided to publish them—revised to date—believing that a practical work, suited to the DAILY REQUIREMENTS OF MODERN ENGINEERS, would be favourably received.*

In the Third Edition, the following among other additions have been made, viz.: Rules for the Proportions of Riveted Joints in Soft Steel Plates, the Results of Experiments by PROFESSOR KENNEDY for the Institution of Mechanical Engineers—Rules for the Proportions of Turbines—Rules for the Strength of Hollow Shafts of Whitworth's Compressed Steel, &c.

** OPINIONS OF THE PRESS.

"The author treats every subject from the point of view of one who has collected workshop notes for application in workshop practice, rather than from the theoretical or literary aspect. The volume contains a great deal of that kind of information which is gained only by practical experience, and is seldom written in books."—*Engineer.*

"The volume is an exceedingly useful one, brimful with engineers' notes, memoranda, and rules, and well worthy of being on every mechanical engineer's bookshelf."—*Mechanical World.*

"A formidable mass of facts and figures, readily accessible through an elaborate index . . . . . Such a volume will be found absolutely necessary as a book of reference in all sorts of 'works' connected with the metal trades."—*Ryland's Iron Trades Circular.*

"Brimful of useful information, stated in a concise form, Mr. Hutton's books have met a pressing want among engineers. The book must prove extremely useful to every practical man possessing a copy."—*Practical Engineer.*

"The Modernised Templeton."

THE PRACTICAL MECHANIC'S WORKSHOP COMPANION. Comprising a great variety of the most useful Rules and Formulæ in Mechanical Science, with numerous Tables of Practical Data and Calculated Results for Facilitating Mechanical Operations. By WILLIAM TEMPLETON, Author of "The Engineer's Practical Assistant," &c. &c. Fifteenth Edition, Revised, Modernised, and considerably Enlarged by WALTER S. HUTTON, C.E., Author of "The Works' Manager's Handbook," "The Practical Engineer's Handbook," &c. Fcap. 8vo, nearly 500 pp., with Eight Plates and upwards of 250 Illustrative Diagrams, 6s., strongly bound for workshop or pocket wear and tear.

☞ TEMPLETON'S "MECHANIC'S WORKSHOP COMPANION" *has been for more than a quarter of a century deservedly popular, and, as the well-worn and thumbmarked vade mecum of several generations of intelligent and aspiring workmen, it has had the reputation of having been the means of raising many of them in their position in life.*

In consequence of the lapse of time since the Author's death, and the great advances in Mechanical Science, the Publishers have thought it advisable to have it entirely Reconstructed and Modernised; and in its present greatly Enlarged and Improved form, they are sure that it will commend itself to the English workmen of the present day all the world over, and become, like its predecessors, their indispensable friend and referee.

A smaller type having been adopted, and the page increased in size, while the number of pages has advanced from about 330 to nearly 500, the book practically contains double the amount of matter that was comprised in the original work.

** OPINIONS OF THE PRESS.

"In its modernised form Hutton's 'Templeton' should have a wide sale, for it contains much valuable information which the mechanic will often find of use, and not a few tables and notes which he might look for in vain in other works. This modernised edition will be appreciated by all who have learned to value the original editions of 'Templeton.'"—*English Mechanic.*

"It has met with great success in the engineering workshop, as we can testify; and there are a great many men who, in a great measure, owe their rise in life to this little book."—*Building News.*

"This familiar text-book—well known to all mechanics and engineers—is of essential service to the every-day requirements of engineers, millwrights, and the various trades connected with engineering and building. The new modernised edition is worth its weight in gold."—*Building News.* (Second Notice.)

"The publishers wisely entrusted the task of revision of this popular, valuable and useful book to Mr. Hutton, than whom a more competent man they could not have found."—*Iron.*

Stone-working Machinery.

STONE-WORKING MACHINERY, and the Rapid and Economical Conversion of Stone. With Hints on the Arrangement and Management of Stone Works. By M. Powis BALE, M.I.M.E. Crown 8vo, 9s.

"Should be in the hands of every mason or student of stone-work."—*Colliery Guardian.*
"It is in every sense of the word a standard work upon a subject which the author is fully competent to deal exhaustively with."—*Builder's Weekly Reporter.*
"A capital handbook for all who manipulate stone for building or ornamental purposes."—*Machinery Market.*

Pump Construction and Management.

PUMPS AND PUMPING : A Handbook for Pump Users. Being Notes on Selection, Construction and Management. By M. Powis BALE, M.I.M.E., Author of "Woodworking Machinery," "Saw Mills," &c. Crown 8vo, 2s. 6d. cloth. [*Just published.*

"The matter is set forth as concisely as possible. In fact, condensation rather than diffuseness has been the author's aim throughout; yet he does not seem to have omitted anything likely to be of use."—*Journal of Gas Lighting.*
"Thoroughly practical and simply and clearly written."—*Glasgow Herald.*

Turning.

LATHE-WORK : A Practical Treatise on the Tools, Appliances, and Processes employed in the Art of Turning. By PAUL N. HASLUCK. Third Edition, Revised and Enlarged. Crown 8vo, 5s. cloth.

"Written by a man who knows, not only how work ought to be done, but who also knows how to do it, and how to convey his knowledge to others. To all turners this book would be valuable."—*Engineering.*
"We can safely recommend the work to young engineers. To the amateur it will simply be invaluable. To the student it will convey a great deal of useful information."—*Engineer.*
"A compact, succinct, and handy guide to lathe-work did not exist in our language until Mr. Hasluck, by the publication of this treatise, gave the turner a true *vade-mecum.*"—*House Decorator.*

Screw-Cutting.

SCREW THREADS : And Methods of Producing Them. With Numerous Tables, and complete directions for using Screw-Cutting Lathes. By PAUL N. HASLUCK, Author of "Lathe-Work," &c. With Fifty Illustrations. Second Edition. Waistcoat-pocket size, price 1s. cloth.

"Full of useful information, hints and practical criticism. Taps, dies and screwing-tools generally are illustrated and their action described."—*Mechanical World.*

Smith's Tables for Mechanics, etc.

TABLES, MEMORANDA, AND CALCULATED RESULTS, FOR MECHANICS, ENGINEERS, ARCHITECTS, BUILDERS, etc. Selected and Arranged by FRANCIS SMITH. Fourth Edition, Revised and Enlarged, 250 pp., waistcoat-pocket size, 1s. 6d. limp leather.

"It would, perhaps, be as difficult to make a small pocket-book selection of notes and formulæ to suit ALL engineers as it would be to make a universal medicine; but Mr. Smith's waistcoat-pocket collection may be looked upon as a successful attempt."—*Engineer.*
"The best example we have ever seen of 250 pages of useful matter packed into the dimensions of a card-case."—*Building News.*   "A veritable pocket treasury of knowledge."—*Iron.*

Engineer's and Machinist's Assistant.

THE ENGINEER'S, MILLWRIGHT'S, and MACHINIST'S PRACTICAL ASSISTANT. A collection of Useful Tables, Rules and Data. By WILLIAM TEMPLETON. 7th Edition, with Additions. 18mo, 2s. 6d. cloth.

"Occupies a foremost place among books of this kind. A more suitable present to an apprentice to any of the mechanical trades could not possibly be made."—*Building News.*
"A deservedly popular work, it should be in the 'drawer' of every mechanic."—*English Mechanic.*

Iron and Steel.

"IRON AND STEEL" : A Work for the Forge, Foundry, Factory, and Office. Containing ready, useful, and trustworthy Information for Ironmasters and their Stock-takers; Managers of Bar, Rail, Plate, and Sheet Rolling Mills; Iron and Metal Founders; Iron Ship and Bridge Builders; Mechanical, Mining, and Consulting Engineers; Architects, Builders, and Draughtsmen. By CHARLES HOARE, Author of "The Slide Rule," &c. Eighth Edition, Revised and considerably Enlarged. 32mo, 6s. leather.

"One of the best of the pocket books."—*English Mechanic.*
"We cordially recommend this book to those engaged in considering the details of all kinds of iron and steel works."—*Naval Science.*

Engineering Construction.

PATTERN-MAKING : *A Practical Treatise,* embracing the Main Types of Engineering Construction. and including Gearing, both Hand and Machine made, Engine Work, Sheaves and Pulleys. Pipes and Columns, Screws. Machine Parts, Pumps and Cocks. the Moulding of Patterns in Loam and Greensand, &c., together with the methods of Estimating the weight of Castings; to which is added an Appendix of Tables for Workshop Reference. By a FOREMAN PATTERN MAKER. With upwards of Three Hundred and Seventy Illustrations. Crown 8vo, 7s. 6d. cloth.

' A well-written technical guide. evidently written by a man who understands and has practised what he has written about. We cordially recommend it to engineering students, young journeymen. and others desirous of being initiated into the mysteries of pattern-making."—*Builder.*

" Likely to prove a welcome guide to many workmen, especially to draughtsmen who have lacked a training in the shops, pupils pursuing their practical studies in our factories, and to employers and managers in engineering works."—*Hardware Trade Journal.*

"More than 370 illustrations help to explain the text, which is however, always clear and explicit, thus rendering the work an excellent *vade mecum* for the apprentice who desires to become master of his trade."—*English Mechanic.*

Dictionary of Mechanical Engineering Terms.

LOCKWOOD'S DICTIONARY OF TERMS USED IN THE *PRACTICE OF MECHANICAL ENGINEERING,* embracing those current in the Drawing Office, Pattern Shop, Foundry. Fitting. Turning. Smith's and Boiler Shops, &c. &c. Comprising upwards of 6,000 Definitions. Edited by A FOREMAN PATTERN-MAKER Author of " Pattern Making." Crown 8vo, 7s. 6d. cloth.

' Just the sort of handy dictionary required by the various trades engaged in mechanical engineering. The practical engineering pupil will find the book of great value in his studies, and every foreman engineer and mechanic should have a copy."—*Building News.*

"After a careful examination of the book and trying all manner of words we think that the engineer will here find all he is likely to require. It will be largely used."—*Practical Engineer.*

"This admirable dictionary, although primarily intended for the use of draughtsmen and other technical craftsmen, is of much larger value as a book of reference and will find a ready welcome in many libraries."—*Glasgow Herald.*

"One of the most useful books which can be presented to a mechanic or student."—*English Mechanic.*

" Not merely a dictionary, but, to a certain extent also a most valuable guide It strikes us as a happy idea to combine with a definition of the phrase useful information on the subject of which it treats."—*Machinery Market.*

" This carefully-compiled volume forms a kind of pocket cyclopædia of the extensive subject to which it is devoted. No word having connection with any branch of constructive engineering seems to be omitted. No more comprehensive work has been, so far, issued."—*Knowledge.*

" We strongly commend this useful and reliable adviser to our friends in the workshop, and to students everywhere."—*Colliery Guardian.*

Steam Boilers.

A TREATISE ON STEAM BOILERS: *Their Strength, Construction, and Economical Working.* By ROBERT WILSON, C.E. Fifth Edition. 12mo, 6s. cloth.

"The best treatise that has ever been published on steam boilers."—*Engineer.*

"The author shows himself perfect master of his subject, and we heartily recommend all employing steam power to possess themselves of the work."—*Ryland's Iron Trade Circular.*

Boiler Chimneys.

BOILER AND FACTORY CHIMNEYS; *Their Draught-Power and Stability.* With a Chapter on *Lightning Conductors.* By ROBERT WILSON, C.E., Author of "A Treatise on Steam Boilers," &c. Second Edition. Crown 8vo, 3s. 6d. cloth.

" Full of useful information, definite in statement, and thoroughly practical in treatment."—*The Local Government Chronicle.*

" A valuable contribution to the literature of scientific building. . . . The whole subject is a very interesting and important one, and it is gratifying to know that it has fallen into such competent hands."—*The Builder.*

Boiler Making.

THE BOILER-MAKER'S READY RECKONER. With Examples of Practical Geometry and Templating, for the Use of Platers, Smiths and Riveters. By JOHN COURTNEY, Edited by D. K. CLARK, M.I.C.E. Second Edition, Revised, with Additions, 12mo, 5s. half-bound.

No workman or apprentice should be without this book."—*Iron Trade Circular.*

" A reliable guide to the working boiler-maker."—*Iron.*

" Boiler-makers will readily recognise the value of this volume. . . . The tables are clearly printed, and so arranged that they can be referred to with the greatest facility, so that it cannot be doubted that they will be generally appreciated and much used."—*Mining Journal.*

Steam Engine.

TEXT-BOOK ON THE STEAM ENGINE. With a Supplement on Gas Engines. By T. M. GOODEVE, M.A., Barrister-at-Law, Author of "The Elements of Mechanism," &c. Tenth Edition, Enlarged. With numerous Illustrations. Crown 8vo, 6s. cloth. [*Just published.*

"Professor Goodeve has given us a treatise on the steam engine which will bear comparison with anything written by Huxley or Maxwell and we can award it no higher praise."—*Engineer.*

"Professor Goodeve's book is ably and clearly written. It is a sound work."—*Athenæum.*

"Mr. Goodeve's text-book is a work of which every young engineer should possess himself.'—*Mining Journal.*

"Essentially practical in its aim. The manner of exposition leaves nothing to be desired.'—*Scotsman.*

Gas Engines.

ON GAS-ENGINES. Being a Reprint, with some Additions, of the Supplement to the *Text-book on the Steam Engine,* by T. M. GOODEVE, M.A. Crown 8vo, 2s. 6d. cloth. [*Just published.*

"Like all Mr. Goodeve's writings, the present is no exception in point of general excellence. It is a valuable little volume."—*Mechanical World.*

"This little book will be useful to those who desire to understand how the gas-engine works.'—*English Mechanic.*

Steam.

THE SAFE USE OF STEAM. Containing Rules for Unprofessional Steam-users. By an ENGINEER. Sixth Edition. Sewed, 6d.

"If steam-users would but learn this little book by heart boiler explosions would become sensations by their rarity."—*English Mechanic.*

Coal and Speed Tables.

A POCKET BOOK OF COAL AND SPEED TABLES, *for Engineers and Steam-users.* By NELSON FOLEY, Author of "Boiler Construction." Pocket-size, 3s. 6d. cloth; 4s. leather.

"This is a very useful book, containing very useful tables. The results given are well chosen, an'l the volume contains evidence that the author really understands his subject. We can recommend the work with pleasure."—*Mechanical World.*

"These tables are designed to meet the requirements of every-day use; they are of sufficient scope for most practical purposes, and may be commended to engineers and users of steam."—*Iron.*

"This pocket-book well merits the attention of the practical engineer. Mr. Foley has compiled a very useful set of tables, the information contained in which is frequently required by engineers, coal consumers and users of steam."—*Iron and Coal Trades Review.*

Fire Engineering.

FIRES, FIRE-ENGINES, AND FIRE-BRIGADES. With a History of Fire-Engines, their Construction, Use, and Management; Remarks on Fire-Proof Buildings, and the Preservation of Life from Fire; Statistics of the Fire Appliances in English Towns; Foreign Fire Systems; Hints on Fire Brigades, &c. &c. By CHARLES F. T. YOUNG, C.E. With numerous Illustrations, 544 pp., demy 8vo, £1 4s. cloth.

"To such of our readers as are interested in the subject of fires and fire apparatus, we can most heartily commend this book. It is really the only English work we now have upon the subject."—*Engineering.*

"It displays much evidence of careful research; and Mr. Young has put his facts neatly together. It is evident enough that his acquaintance with the practical details of the construction of steam fire engines, old and new, and the conditions with which it is necessary they should comply, is accurate and full."—*Engineer.*

Gas Lighting.

COMMON SENSE FOR GAS-USERS: A *Catechism of Gas-Lighting for Householders, Gasfitters, Millowners, Architects, Engineers, etc.* By ROBERT WILSON, C.E., Author of "A Treatise on Steam Boilers." Second Edition, with Folding Plates and Wood Engravings. Crown 8vo, price 1s. in wrapper.

"All gas-users will decidedly benefit, both in pocket and comfort, if they will avail themselves of Mr. Wilson's counsels."—*Engineering.*

Dynamo Construction.

HOW TO MAKE A DYNAMO: A *Practical Treatise for Amateurs.* Containing numerous Illustrations and Detailed Instructions for Constructing a Small Dynamo, to Produce the Electric Light. By ALFRED CROFTS. Second Edition, Revised and Enlarged. Crown 8vo, 2s. cloth. [*Just published.*

"The instructions given in this unpretentious little book are sufficiently clear and explicit to enable any amateur mechanic possessed of average skill and the usual tools to be found in an amateur's workshop, to build a practical dynamo machine.'—*Electrician.*

THE POPULAR WORKS OF MICHAEL REYNOLDS
("THE ENGINE DRIVER'S FRIEND").

Locomotive-Engine Driving.

LOCOMOTIVE-ENGINE DRIVING: A Practical Manual for Engineers in charge of Locomotive Engines. By MICHAEL REYNOLDS, Member of the Society of Engineers, formerly Locomotive Inspector L. B. and S. C. R. Eighth Edition. Including a KEY TO THE LOCOMOTIVE ENGINE. With Illustrations and Portrait of Author. Crown 8vo, 4s. 6d. cloth.

"Mr. Reynolds has supplied a want, and has supplied it well. We can confidently recommend the book, not only to the practical driver, but to everyone who takes an interest in the performance of locomotive engines."—The Engineer.

"Mr. Reynolds has opened a new chapter in the literature of the day. This admirable practical treatise, of the practical utility of which we have to speak in terms of warm commendation."—Athenæum.

"Evidently the work of one who knows his subject thoroughly."—Railway Service Gazette.

"Were the cautions and rules given in the book to become part of the every-day working of our engine-drivers, we might have fewer distressing accidents to deplore."—Scotsman.

Stationary Engine Driving.

STATIONARY ENGINE DRIVING: A Practical Manual for Engineers in charge of Stationary Engines. By MICHAEL REYNOLDS. Third Edition, Enlarged. With Plates and Woodcuts. Crown 8vo, 4s. cloth.

"The author is thoroughly acquainted with his subjects, and his advice on the various points treated is clear and practical. . . . He has produced a manual which is an exceedingly useful one for the class for whom it is specially intended."—Engineering.

"Our author leaves no stone unturned. He is determined that his readers shall not only know something about the stationary engine, but all about it."—Engineer.

"An engineman who has mastered the contents of Mr. Reynolds's book will require but little actual experience with boilers and engines before he can be trusted to look after them."—English Mechanic.

The Engineer, Fireman, and Engine-Boy.

THE MODEL LOCOMOTIVE ENGINEER, FIREMAN, and ENGINE-BOY. Comprising a Historical Notice of the Pioneer Locomotive Engines and their Inventors. By MICHAEL REYNOLDS. With numerous Illustrations and a fine Portrait of George Stephenson. Crown 8vo, 4s. 6d. cloth.

"From the technical knowledge of the author it will appeal to the railway man of to-day more forcibly than anything written by Dr. Smiles. . . . The volume contains information of a technical kind, and facts that every driver should be familiar with."—English Mechanic.

"We should be glad to see this book in the possession of everyone in the kingdom who has ever laid, or is to lay, hands on a locomotive engine."—Iron.

Continuous Railway Brakes.

CONTINUOUS RAILWAY BRAKES: A Practical Treatise on the several Systems in Use in the United Kingdom; their Construction and Performance. With copious Illustrations and numerous Tables. By MICHAEL REYNOLDS. Large crown 8vo, 9s. cloth.

"A popular explanation of the different brakes. It will be of great assistance in forming public opinion, and will be studied with benefit by those who take an interest in the brake."—English Mechanic.

"Written with sufficient technical detail to enable the principle and relative connection of the various parts of each particular brake to be readily grasped."—Mechanical World.

Engine-Driving Life.

ENGINE-DRIVING LIFE: Stirring Adventures and Incidents in the Lives of Locomotive-Engine Drivers. By MICHAEL REYNOLDS. Second Edition, with Additional Chapters. Crown 8vo, 2s. cloth.   [Just published.

"From first to last perfectly fascinating. Wilkie Collins's most thrilling conceptions are thrown into the shade by true incidents, endless in their variety, related in every page."—North British Mail.

"Anyone who wishes to get a real insight into railway life cannot do better than read 'Engine-Driving Life' for himself; and if he once take it up he will find that the author's enthusiasm and real love of the engine-driving profession will carry him on till he has read every page."—Saturday Review.

Pocket Companion for Enginemen.

THE ENGINEMAN'S POCKET COMPANION AND PRACTICAL EDUCATOR FOR ENGINEMEN, BOILER ATTENDANTS, AND MECHANICS. By MICHAEL REYNOLDS. With Forty-five Illustrations and numerous Diagrams. Second Edition, Revised. Royal 18mo, 3s. 6d., strongly bound for pocket wear.

"This admirable work is well suited to accomplish its object, being the honest workmanship of a competent engineer."—Glasgow Herald.

"A most meritorious work, giving in a succinct and practical form all the information an engine-minder desirous of mastering the scientific principles of his daily calling would require."—Miller.

"A boon to those who are striving to become efficient mechanics."—Daily Chronicle.

French-English Glossary for Engineers, etc.

A POCKET GLOSSARY of TECHNICAL TERMS: ENGLISH-FRENCH, FRENCH-ENGLISH; with Tables suitable for the Architectural, Engineering, Manufacturing and Nautical Professions. By JOHN JAMES FLETCHER, Engineer and Surveyor; 200 pp. Waistcoat-pocket size, 1s. 6d., limp leather.

"It ought certainly to be in the waistcoat-pocket of every professional man. —*Iron*.
"It is a very great advantage for readers and correspondents in France and England to have so large a number of the words relating to engineering and manufacturers collected in a liliputian volume. The little book will be useful both to students and travellers."—*Architect*.
"The glossary of terms is very complete, and many of the tables are new and well arranged. We cordially commend the book."—*Mechanical World*.

Portable Engines.

THE PORTABLE ENGINE; ITS CONSTRUCTION AND MANAGEMENT. A Practical Manual for Owners and Users of Steam Engines generally. By WILLIAM DYSON WANSBROUGH. With 90 Illustrations. Crown 8vo, 3s. 6d. cloth.

"This is a work of value to those who use steam machinery. . . . Should be read by every-one who has a steam engine, on a farm or elsewhere."—*Mark Lane Express*.
"We cordially commend this work to buyers and owners of steam engines, and to those who have to do with their construction or use."—*Timber Trades Journal*.
"Such a general knowledge of the steam engine as Mr. Wansbrough furnishes to the reader should be acquired by all intelligent owners and others who use the steam engine."—*Building News*.

CIVIL ENGINEERING, SURVEYING, etc.

MR. HUMBER'S IMPORTANT ENGINEERING BOOKS.

The Water Supply of Cities and Towns.

A COMPREHENSIVE TREATISE on the WATER-SUPPLY OF CITIES AND TOWNS. By WILLIAM HUMBER, A-M.Inst.C.E., and M. Inst. M.E., Author of "Cast and Wrought Iron Bridge Construction," &c. &c. Illustrated with 50 Double Plates, 1 Single Plate, Coloured Frontispiece, and upwards of 250 Woodcuts, and containing 400 pages of Text. Imp. 4to, £6 6s. elegantly and substantially half-bound in morocco.

List of Contents.

I. Historical Sketch of some of the means that have been adopted for the Supply of Water to Cities and Towns.—II. Water and the Foreign Matter usually associated with it.—III. Rainfall and Evaporation.—IV. Springs and the water-bearing formations of various districts.—V. Measurement and Estimation of the flow of Water.—VI. On the Selection of the Source of Supply.—VII. Wells.—VIII. Reservoirs.—IX. The Purification of Water.—X. Pumps. — XI. Pumping Machinery. — XII. Conduits.—XIII. Distribution of Water.—XIV. Meters, Service Pipes, and House Fittings.—XV. The Law and Economy of Water Works. XVI. Constant and Intermittent Supply.—XVII. Description of Plates. — Appendices, giving Tables of Rates of Supply, Velocities, &c. &c., together with Specifications of several Works illustrated, among which will be found: Aberdeen, Bideford, Canterbury, Dundee, Halifax, Lambeth, Rotherham, Dublin, and others.

"The most systematic and valuable work upon water supply hitherto produced in English, or in any other language. . . . Mr. Humber's work is characterised almost throughout by an exhaustiveness much more distinctive of French and German than of English technical treatises."—*Engineer*.
"We can congratulate Mr. Humber on having been able to give so large an amount of information on a subject so important as the water supply of cities and towns. The plates, fifty in number, are mostly drawings of executed works, and alone would have commanded the attention of every engineer whose practice may lie in this branch of the profession."—*Builder*.

Cast and Wrought Iron Bridge Construction.

A COMPLETE AND PRACTICAL TREATISE ON CAST AND WROUGHT IRON BRIDGE CONSTRUCTION, including Iron Foundations. In Three Parts—Theoretical, Practical, and Descriptive. By WILLIAM HUMBER, A.M.Inst.C.E., and M.Inst.M.E. Third Edition, Revised and much improved, with 115 Double Plates (20 of which now first appear in this edition), and numerous Additions to the Text. In Two Vols., imp. 4to, £6 16s. 6d. half-bound in morocco.

"A very valuable contribution to the standard literature of civil engineering. In addition to elevations, plans and sections, large scale details are given which very much enhance the instructive worth of those illustrations."—*Civil Engineer and Architect's Journal*.
"Mr. Humber's stately volumes, lately issued—in which the most important bridges erected during the last five years, under the direction of the late Mr. Brunel, Sir W. Cubitt, Mr. Hawkshaw, Mr. Page, Mr. Fowler, Mr. Hemans, and others among our most eminent engineers, are drawn and specified in great detail."—*Engineer*.

MR. HUMBER'S GREAT WORK ON MODERN ENGINEERING.

Complete in Four Volumes, imperial 4to, price £12 12s., half-morocco. Each Volume sold separately as follows:—

A RECORD OF THE PROGRESS OF MODERN ENGINEER-
ING. First Series. Comprising Civil, Mechanical, Marine, Hydraulic, Railway, Bridge, and other Engineering Works, &c. By WILLIAM HUMBER, A-M.Inst.C.E., &c. Imp. 4to, with 36 Double Plates, drawn to a large scale, Photographic Portrait of John Hawkshaw, C.E., F.R.S., &c., and copious descriptive Letterpress, Specifications, &c., £3 3s. half-morocco.

List of the Plates and Diagrams.

Victoria Station and Roof, L. B. & S. C. R. (8 plates); Southport Pier (2 plates); Victoria Station and Roof, L. C. & D. and G. W. R. (6 plates); Roof of Cremorne Music Hall; Bridge over G. N. Railway; Roof of Station, Dutch Rhenish Rail (2 plates); Bridge over the Thames, West London Extension Railway (5 plates); Armour Plates; Suspension Bridge, Thames (4 plates); The Allen Engine; Suspension Bridge, Avon (3 plates); Underground Railway (3 plates).

" Handsomely lithographed and printed. It will find favour with many who desire to preserve in a permanent form copies of the plans and specifications prepared for the guidance of the contractors for many important engineering works."—*Engineer.*

HUMBER'S RECORD OF MODERN ENGINEERING. Second
Series. Imp. 4to, with 36 Double Plates, Photographic Portrait of Robert Stephenson, C.E., M.P., F.R.S., &c., and copious descriptive Letterpress, Specifications, &c., £3 3s. half-morocco.

List of the Plates and Diagrams.

Birkenhead Docks, Low Water Basin (15 plates); Charing Cross Station Roof, C. C. Railway (3 plates); Digswell Viaduct, Great Northern Railway; Robbery Wood Viaduct, Great Northern Railway; Iron Permanent Way; Clydach Viaduct, Merthyr, Tredegar, and Abergavenny Railway; Ebbw Viaduct. Merthyr, Tredegar, and Abergavenny Railway; College Wood Viaduct, Cornwall Railway; Dublin Winter Palace Roof (3 plates); Bridge over the Thames, L. C. & D. Railway (6 plates); Albert Harbour, Greenock (4 plates).

" Mr. Humber has done the profession good and true service, by the fine collection of examples he has here brought before the profession and the public."—*Practical Mechanic's Journal.*

HUMBER'S RECORD OF MODERN ENGINEERING. Third
Series. Imp. 4to, with 40 Double Plates, Photographic Portrait of J. R. M'Clean, late Pres. Inst. C.E., and copious descriptive Letterpress, Specifications, &c., £3 3s. half-morocco.

List of the Plates and Diagrams.

MAIN DRAINAGE, METROPOLIS.—*North Side.*—Map showing Interception of Sewers; Middle Level Sewer (2 plates); Outfall Sewer, Bridge over River Lea (3 plates); Outfall Sewer, Bridge over Marsh Lane, North Woolwich Railway, and Bow and Barking Railway Junction; Outfall Sewer, Bridge over Bow and Barking Railway (3 plates); Outfall Sewer, Bridge over East London Waterworks' Feeder (2 plates); Outfall Sewer, Reservoir (2 plates); Outfall Sewer, Tumbling Bay and Outlet; Outfall Sewer, Penstocks, *South Side.*—Outfall Sewer, Bermondsey Branch (2 plates); Outfall Sewer, Reservoir and Outlet (4 plates); Outfall Sewer, Filth Hoist; Sections of Sewers (North and South Sides). THAMES EMBANKMENT.—Section of River Wall; Steamboat Pier, Westminster (2 plates); Landing Stairs between Charing Cross and Waterloo Bridges; York Gate (2 plates); Overflow and Outlet at Savoy Street Sewer (3 plates); Steamboat Pier, Waterloo Bridge (3 plates); Junction of Sewers, Plans and Sections; Gullies, Plans and Sections; Rolling Stock; Granite and Iron Forts.

" The drawings have a constantly increasing value, and whoever desires to possess clear representations of the two great works carried out by our Metropolitan Board will obtain Mr. Humber's volume."—*Engineer.*

HUMBER'S RECORD OF MODERN ENGINEERING. Fourth
Series. Imp. 4to, with 36 Double Plates, Photographic Portrait of John Fowler, late Pres. Inst. C.E., and copious descriptive Letterpress, Specifications, &c., £3 3s. half-morocco.

List of the Plates and Diagrams.

Abbey Mills Pumping Station, Main Drainage, Metropolis (4 plates); Barrow Docks (5 plates); Manquis Viaduct, Santiago and Valparaiso Railway (2 plates); Adam's Locomotive, St. Helen's Canal Railway (2 plates); Cannon Street Station Roof, Charing Cross Railway (3 plates); Road Bridge over the River Moka (2 plates); Telegraphic Apparatus for Mesopotamia; Viaduct over the River Wye, Midland Railway (3 plates); St. Germans Viaduct, Cornwall Railway (2 plates); Wrought-Iron Cylinder for Diving Bell; Millwall Docks (6 plates); Milroy's Patent Excavator; Metropolitan District Railway (6 plates); Harbours, Ports, and Breakwaters (3 plates).

" We gladly welcome another year's issue of this valuable publication from the able pen of Mr. Humber. The accuracy and general excellence of this work are well known, while its useful ness in giving the measurements and details of some of the latest examples of engineering, as carried out by the most eminent men in the profession, cannot be too highly prized."—*Artisan.*

MR. HUMBER'S ENGINEERING BOOKS—*continued.*

Strains, Calculation of.

A HANDY BOOK FOR THE CALCULATION OF STRAINS IN GIRDERS AND SIMILAR STRUCTURES, AND THEIR STRENGTH. Consisting of Formulæ and Corresponding Diagrams, with numerous details for Practical Application, &c. By WILLIAM HUMBER, A-M.Inst.C.E., &c. Fourth Edition. Crown 8vo, nearly 100 Woodcuts and 3 Plates, 7s. 6d. cloth.

" The formulæ are neatly expressed, and the diagrams good."—*Athenæum.*
" We heartily commend this really *handy* book to our engineer and architect readers."—*English Mechanic.*

Barlow's Strength of Materials, enlarged by Humber

A TREATISE ON THE STRENGTH OF MATERIALS; with Rules for Application in Architecture, the Construction of Suspension Bridges, Railways, &c. By PETER BARLOW, F.R.S. A New Edition, revised by his Sons, P. W. BARLOW, F.R.S., and W. H. BARLOW, F.R.S.; to which are added, Experiments by HODGKINSON, FAIRBAIRN, and KIRKALDY; and Formulæ for Calculating Girders, &c. Arranged and Edited by W. HUMBER, A-M.Inst.C.E. Demy 8vo, 400 pp., with 19 large Plates and numerous Woodcuts, 18s. cloth.

" Valuable alike to the student, tyro, and the experienced practitioner. It will always rank in future, as it has hitherto done, as the standard treatise on that particular subject."—*Engineer.*
" There is no greater authority than Barlow."—*Building News.*
" As a scientific work of the first class, it deserves a foremost place on the bookshelves of every civil engineer and practical mechanic."—*English Mechanic.*

Trigonometrical Surveying.

AN OUTLINE OF THE METHOD OF CONDUCTING A TRIGONOMETRICAL SURVEY, for the Formation of Geographical and Topographical Maps and Plans, Military Reconnaissance, Levelling, &c., with Useful Problems, Formulæ, and Tables. By Lieut.-General FROME, R.E. Fourth Edition, Revised and partly Re-written by Major General Sir CHARLES WARREN, G.C.M.G., R.E. With 19 Plates and 115 Woodcuts, royal 8vo, 16s. cloth.

" The simple fact that a fourth edition has been called for is the best testimony to its merits. No words of praise from us can strengthen the position so well and so steadily maintained by this work. Sir Charles Warren has revised the entire work, and made such additions as were necessary to bring every portion of the contents up to the present date."—*Broad Arrow.*

Oblique Bridges.

A PRACTICAL AND THEORETICAL ESSAY ON OBLIQUE BRIDGES. With 13 large Plates. By the late GEORGE WATSON BUCK, M.I.C.E. Third Edition, revised by his Son, J. H. WATSON BUCK, M.I.C.E.; and with the addition of Description to Diagrams for Facilitating the Construction of Oblique Bridges, by W. H. BARLOW, M.I.C.E. Royal 8vo, 12s. cloth.

" The standard text-book for all engineers regarding skew arches is Mr. Buck's treatise, and it would be impossible to consult a better."—*Engineer.*
" Mr. Buck's treatise is recognised as a standard text-book, and his treatment has divested the subject of many of the intricacies supposed to belong to it. As a guide to the engineer and architect, on a confessedly difficult subject, Mr. Buck's work is unsurpassed."—*Building News.*

Water Storage, Conveyance and Utilisation.

WATER ENGINEERING: A Practical Treatise on the Measurement, Storage, Conveyance and Utilisation of Water for the Supply of Towns, for Mill Power, and for other Purposes. By CHARLES SLAGG, Water and Drainage Engineer, A.M.Inst.C.E., Author of "Sanitary Work in the Smaller Towns, and in Villages," &c. With numerous Illustrations. Crown 8vo, 7s. 6d. cloth. [*Just published.*

" As a small practical treatise on the water supply of towns, and on some applications of water-power, the work is in many respects exellent."—*Engineering.*
" The author has collated the results deduced from the experiments of the most eminent authorities, and has presented them in a compact and practical form, accompanied by very clear and detailed explanations. . . . The application of water as a motive power is treated very carefully and exhaustively."—*Builder.*
" For anyone who desires to begin the study of hydraulics with a consideration of the practical applications of the science there is no better guide."—*Architect.*

Statics, Graphic and Analytic.

GRAPHIC AND ANALYTIC STATICS, *in their Practical Appli-cation to the Treatment of Stresses in Roofs, Solid Girders, Lattice, Bowstring and Suspension Bridges, Braced Iron Arches and Piers, and other Frameworks.* By R. HUDSON GRAHAM, C.E. Containing Diagrams and Plates to Scale. With numerous Examples, many taken from existing Structures. Specially arranged for Class-work in Colleges and Universities. Second Edition, Revised and Enlarged. 8vo, 16s. cloth.

"Mr. Graham's book will find a place wherever graphic and analytic statics are used or studied.' —*Engineer.*
"The work is excellent from a practical point of view, and has evidently been prepared with much care. The directions for working are ample, and are illustrated by an abundance of well-selected examples. It is an excellent text-book for the practical draughtsman."—*Athenæum.*

Student's Text-Book on Surveying.

PRACTICAL SURVEYING : A Text-Book for Students pre-paring for Examination or for Survey-work in the Colonies. By GEORGE W. USILL, A.M.I.C.E., Author of "The Statistics of the Water Supply of Great Britain." With Four Lithographic Plates and upwards of 330 Illustrations. Crown 8vo, 7s. 6d. cloth. [*Just published.*

"The best forms of instruments are described as to their construction, uses and modes of employment, and there are innumerable hints on work and equipment such as the author, in his experience as surveyor, draughtsman and teacher, has found necessary, and which the student in his inexperience will find most serviceable."—*Engineer.*
"We have no hesitation in saying that the student will find this treatise a better guide than any of its predecessors. . . . It deserves to be recognised as the first book which should be put in the hands of a pupil of Civil Engineering, and every gentleman of education who sets out for the Colonies would find it well to have a copy."—*Architect.*
"A very useful, practical handbook on field practice. Clear, accurate and not too condensed."—*Journal of Education.*

Survey Practice.

AID TO SURVEY PRACTICE, *for Reference in Surveying, Level-ling, Setting-out and in Route Surveys of Travellers by Land and Sea.* With Tables, Illustrations, and Records. By LOWIS D'A. JACKSON, A.M.I.C.E., Author of "Hydraulic Manual," "Modern Metrology," &c. Second Edition, Enlarged. Large crown 8vo, 12s. 6d. cloth.

"Mr. Jackson has produced a valuable *vade-mecum* for the surveyor. We can recommend this book as containing an admirable supplement to the teaching of the accomplished surveyor."—*Athenæum.*
"As a text-book we should advise all surveyors to place it in their libraries, and study well the matured instructions afforded in its pages."—*Colliery Guardian.*
"The author brings to his work a fortunate union of theory and practical experience which, aided by a clear and lucid style of writing, renders the book a very useful one."—*Builder.*

Surveying, Land and Marine.

LAND AND MARINE SURVEYING, in Reference to the Pre-paration of Plans for Roads and Railways; Canals, Rivers, Towns' Water Supplies; Docks and Harbours. With Description and Use of Surveying Instruments. By W. D. HASKOLL, C.E., Author of "Bridge and Viaduct Construction," &c. Second Edition, with Additions. Large crown 8vo, 9s. cloth.

"This book must prove of great value to the student. We have no hesitation in recommend-ing it, feeling assured that it will more than repay a careful study."—*Mechanical World.*
"We can strongly recommend it as a carefully-written and valuable text-book. It enjoys a well-deserved repute among surveyors."—*Builder.*
"This volume cannot fail to prove of the utmost practical utility. It may be safely recommended to all students who aspire to become clean and expert surveyors."—*Mining Journal.*

Tunnelling.

PRACTICAL TUNNELLING. Explaining in detail the Setting-out of the works, Shaft-sinking and Heading-driving, Ranging the Lines and Levelling underground, Sub-Excavating, Timbering, and the Construction of the Brickwork of Tunnels, with the amount of Labour required for, and the Cost of, the various portions of the work. By FREDERICK W. SIMMS, F.G.S., M.Inst.C.E. Third Edition, Revised and Extended by D. KINNEAR CLARK, M.Inst.C.E. ; Imperial 8vo, with 21 Folding Plates and numerous Wood Engravings, 30s. cloth.

"The estimation in which Mr. Simms's book on tunnelling has been held for over thirty years cannot be more truly expressed than in the words of the late Prof. Rankine :—'The best source of in-formation on the subject of tunnels is Mr. F. W. Simms's work on Practical Tunnelling.'"—*Architect.*
"It has been regarded from the first as a text book of the subject. . . . Mr. Clarke has added immensely to the value of the book."—*Engineer.*

Levelling.

A TREATISE ON THE PRINCIPLES AND PRACTICE OF LEVELLING. Showing its Application to purposes of Railway and Civil Engineering, in the Construction of Roads; with Mr. TELFORD's Rules for the same. By FREDERICK W. SIMMS, F.G.S., M.Inst.C.E.   Seventh Edition, with the addition of LAW's Practical Examples for Setting-out Railway Curves, and TRAUTWINE's Field Practice of Laying-out Circular Curves.   With 7 Plates and numerous Woodcuts, 8vo, 8s. 6d. cloth.   *** TRAUTWINE on Curves may be had separate, 5s.

" The text-book on levelling in most of our engineering schools and colleges."—*Engineer.*
" The publishers have rendered a substantial service to the profession, especially to the younger members, by bringing out the present edition of Mr. Simms's useful work."—*Engineering.*

Heat, Expansion by.

EXPANSION OF STRUCTURES BY HEAT. By JOHN KEILY, C.E., late of the Indian Public Works and Victorian Railway Departments. Crown 8vo, 3s. cloth.

SUMMARY OF CONTENTS.

Section I. FORMULAS AND DATA.	Section VI. MECHANICAL FORCE OF
Section II. METAL BARS.	HEAT.
Section III. SIMPLE FRAMES.	Section VII. WORK OF EXPANSION
Section IV. COMPLEX FRAMES AND	AND CONTRACTION.
PLATES.	Section VIII. SUSPENSION BRIDGES.
Section V. THERMAL CONDUCTIVITY.	Section IX. MASONRY STRUCTURES.

" The aim the author has set before him, viz., to show the effects of heat upon metallic and other structures, is a laudable one, for this is a branch of physics upon which the engineer or architect can find but little reliable and comprehensive data in books."—*Builder.*
" Whoever is concerned to know the effect of changes of temperature on such structures as suspension bridges and the like, could not do better than consult Mr. Keily's valuable and handy exposition of the geometrical principles involved in these changes."—*Scotsman.*

Practical Mathematics.

MATHEMATICS FOR PRACTICAL MEN: Being a Commonplace Book of Pure and Mixed Mathematics. Designed chiefly for the use of Civil Engineers, Architects and Surveyors. By OLINTHUS GREGORY, LL.D., F.R.A.S., Enlarged by HENRY LAW, C.E.   4th Edition, carefully Revised by J. R. YOUNG, formerly Professor of Mathematics, Belfast College. With 13 Plates, 8vo, £1 1s. cloth.

" The engineer or architect will here find ready to his hand rules for solving nearly every mathematical difficulty that may arise in his practice   The rules are in all cases explained by means of examples, in which every step of the process is clearly worked out."—*Builder.*
" It is an instructive book for the student, and a text-book for him who, having once mastered the subjects it treats of, needs occasionally to refresh his memory upon them."—*Building News.*

Hydraulic Tables.

HYDRAULIC TABLES, CO-EFFICIENTS, and FORMULÆ for finding the Discharge of Water from Orifices, Notches, Weirs, Pipes, and Rivers. With New Formulæ, Tables, and General Information on Rainfall, Catchment-Basins, Drainage, Sewerage, Water Supply for Towns and Mill Power. By JOHN NEVILLE, Civil Engineer, M.R.I.A.   Third Edition, carefully Revised, with Additions. Numerous Illustrations.   Cr. 8vo, 14s. cloth.

" Alike valuable to students and engineers in practice; its study will prevent the annoyance of avoidable failures, and assist them to select the readiest means of successfully carrying out any given work connected with hydraulic engineering."—*Mining Journal.*
" It is, of all English books on the subject, the one nearest to completeness. . . . From the good arrangement of the matter, the clear explanations, and abundance of formulæ, the carefully calculated tables, and, above all, the thorough acquaintance with both theory and construction, which is displayed from first to last, the book will be found to be an acquisition."—*Architect.*

Hydraulics.

HYDRAULIC MANUAL. Consisting of Working Tables and Explanatory Text. Intended as a Guide in Hydraulic Calculations and Field Operations. By LOWIS D'A. JACKSON, Author of "Aid to Survey Practice," " Modern Metrology," &c.   Fourth Edition, Enlarged.   Large cr. 8vo, 16s. cl.

" The author has had a wide experience in hydraulic engineering and has been a careful observer of the facts which have come under his notice, and from the great mass of material at his command he has constructed a manual which may be accepted as a trustworthy guide to this branch of the engineer's profession.   We can heartily recommend this volume to all who desire to be acquainted with the latest development of this important subject."—*Engineering.*
" The most useful feature of this work is its freedom from what is superannuated, and its thorough adoption of recent experiments; the text is, in fact, in great part a short account of the great modern experiments."—*Nature.*

Drainage.

ON THE DRAINAGE OF LANDS, TOWNS AND BUILD-INGS. By G. D. DEMPSEY, C.E., Author of "The Practical Railway Engineer," &c. Revised, with large Additions on RECENT PRACTICE IN DRAINAGE ENGINEERING, by D. KINNEAR CLARK, M.Inst.C.E. Author of "Tramways : Their Construction and Working," "A Manual of Rules, Tables, and Data for Mechanical Engineers," &c. &c. Crown 8vo, 7s. 6d. cloth.

"The new matter added to Mr. Dempsey's excellent work is characterised by the comprehensive grasp and accuracy of detail for which the name of Mr. D. K. Clark is a sufficient voucher."—*Athenæum.*
"As a work on recent practice in drainage engineering, the book is to be commended to all who are making that branch of engineering science their special study."—*Iron.*
"A comprehensive manual on drainage engineering, and a useful introduction to the student." *Building News.*

Tramways and their Working.

TRAMWAYS : THEIR CONSTRUCTION AND WORKING. Embracing a Comprehensive History of the System ; with an exhaustive Analysis of the various Modes of Traction, including Horse-Power, Steam, Heated Water, and Compressed Air ; a Description of the Varieties of Rolling Stock ; and ample Details of Cost and Working Expenses : the Progress recently made in Tramway Construction, &c. &c. By D. KINNEAR CLARK, M.Inst.C.E. With over 200 Wood Engravings, and 13 Folding Plates. Two Vols., large crown 8vo, 30s. cloth.

"All interested in tramways must refer to it, as all railway engineers have turned to the author's work 'Railway Machinery.'"—*Engineer.*
"An exhaustive and practical work on tramways, in which the history of this kind of locomotion, and a description and cost of the various modes of laying tramways, are to be found."—*Building News.*
"The best form of rails, the best mode of construction, and the best mechanical appliances are so fairly indicated in the work under review, that any engineer about to construct a tramway will be enabled at once to obtain the practical information which will be of most service to him."—*Athenæum.*

Oblique Arches.

A PRACTICAL TREATISE ON THE CONSTRUCTION OF OBLIQUE ARCHES. By JOHN HART. Third Edition, with Plates. Imperial 8vo, 8s. cloth.

Curves, Tables for Setting-out.

TABLES OF TANGENTIAL ANGLES AND MULTIPLES for Setting-out Curves from 5 to 200 Radius. By ALEXANDER BEAZELEY, M.Inst.C.E. Third Edition. Printed on 48 Cards, and sold in a cloth box, waistcoat-pocket size, 3s. 6d.

"Each table is printed on a small card, which, being placed on the theodolite, leaves the hands free to manipulate the instrument—no small advantage as regards the rapidity of work."—*Engineer.*
"Very handy ; a man may know that all his day's work must fall on two of these cards, which he puts into his own card-case, and leaves the rest behind."—*Athenæum.*

Earthwork.

EARTHWORK TABLES. Showing the Contents in Cubic Yards of Embankments, Cuttings, &c., of Heights or Depths up to an average of 80 feet. By JOSEPH BROADBENT, C.E., and FRANCIS CAMPIN, C.E. Crown 8vo, 5s. cloth.

"The way in which accuracy is attained, by a simple division of each cross section into three elements, two in which are constant and one variable, is ingenious."—*Athenæum.*

Tunnel Shafts.

THE CONSTRUCTION OF LARGE TUNNEL SHAFTS : A Practical and Theoretical Essay. By J. H. WATSON BUCK, M.Inst.C.E., Resident Engineer, London and North-Western Railway. Illustrated with Folding Plates, royal 8vo, 12s. cloth.

"Many of the methods given are of extreme practical value to the mason ; and the observations on the form of arch, the rules for ordering the stone, and the construction of the templates will be found of considerable use. We commend the book to the engineering profession."—*Building News.*
"Will be regarded by civil engineers as of the utmost value, and calculated to save much time and obviate many mistakes."—*Colliery Guardian.*

Girders, Strength of.

GRAPHIC TABLE FOR FACILITATING THE COMPUTATION OF THE WEIGHTS OF WROUGHT IRON AND STEEL GIRDERS, etc., for Parliamentary and other Estimates. By J. H. WATSON BUCK, M.Inst.C.E On a Sheet, 2s.6d.

River Engineering.

RIVER BARS: *The Causes of their Formation, and their Treatment by " Induced Tidal Scour;"* with a Description of the Successful Reduction by this Method of the Bar at Dublin. By A. J. MANN, Assist. Eng, to the Dublin Port and Docks Board. Royal 8vo, 7s. 6d. cloth.

" We recommend all interested in harbour works—and, indeed, those concerned in the improvements of rivers generally—to read Mr. Mann's interesting work on the treatment of river bars."—*Engineer.*

Trusses.

TRUSSES OF WOOD AND IRON. *Practical Applications of Science in Determining the Stresses, Breaking Weights, Safe Loads, Scantlings, and Details of Construction,* with Complete Working Drawings. By WILLIAM GRIFFITHS, Surveyor, Assistant Master, Tranmere School of Science and Art. Oblong 8vo, 4s. 6d. cloth.

" This handy little book enters so minutely into every detail connected with the construction roof trusses, that no student need be ignorant of these matters."—*Practical Engineer.*

Railway Working.

SAFE RAILWAY WORKING. *A Treatise on Railway Accidents: Their Cause and Prevention; with a Description of Modern Appliances and Systems.* By CLEMENT E. STRETTON, C.E., Vice-President and Consulting Engineer, Amalgamated Society of Railway Servants. With Illustrations and Coloured Plates, crown 8vo, 4s. 6d. strongly bound.

" A book for the engineer, the directors, the managers; and, in short, all who wish for information on railway matters will find a perfect encyclopædia in ' Safe Railway Working.' "—*Railway Review.*
" We commend the remarks on railway signalling to all railway managers, especially where a uniform code and practice is advocated."—*Herepath's Railway Journal.*
" The author may be congratulated on having collected, in a very convenient form, much valuable information on the principal questions affecting the safe working of railways."—*Railway Engineer.*

Field-Book for Engineers.

THE ENGINEER'S, MINING SURVEYOR'S, AND CONTRACTOR'S FIELD-BOOK. Consisting of a Series of Tables, with Rules, Explanations of Systems, and use of Theodolite for Traverse Surveying and Plotting the Work with minute accuracy by means of Straight Edge and Set Square only; Levelling with the Theodolite, Casting-out and Reducing Levels to Datum, and Plotting Sections in the ordinary manner; setting-out Curves with the Theodolite by Tangential Angles and Multiples, with Right and Left-hand Readings of the Instrument: Setting-out Curves without Theodolite, on the System of Tangential Angles by sets of Tangents and Offsets; and Earthwork Tables to 80 feet deep, calculated for every 6 inches in depth. By W. DAVIS HASKOLL, C.E. With numerous Woodcuts. Fourth Edition, Enlarged. Crown 8vo, 12s. cloth.

' The book is very handy; the separate tables of sines and tangents to every minute will make it useful for many other purposes, the genuine traverse tables existing all the same."—*Athenæum*
" Every person engaged in engineering field operations will estimate the importance of such a work and the amount of valuable time which will be saved by reference to a set of reliable tables prepared with the accuracy and fulness of those given in this volume."—*Railway News.*

Earthwork, Measurement of.

A MANUAL ON EARTHWORK. By ALEX. J. S. GRAHAM, C.E. With numerous Diagrams. 18mo, 2s. 6d. cloth.

" A great amount of practical information, very admirably arranged, and available for rough estimates, as well as for the more exact calculations required in the engineer's and contractor's offices."—*Artizan.*

Strains in Ironwork.

THE STRAINS ON STRUCTURES OF IRONWORK; with Practical Remarks on Iron Construction. By F. W. SHEILDS, M.Inst.C.E. Second Edition, with 5 Plates. Royal 8vo, 5s. cloth.

" The student cannot find a better little book on this subject."—*Engineer.*

Cast Iron and other Metals, Strength of.

A PRACTICAL ESSAY ON THE STRENGTH OF CAST IRON AND OTHER METALS. By THOMAS TREDGOLD, C.E. Fifth Edition, including HODGKINSON'S Experimental Researches. 8vo, 12s. cloth.

ARCHITECTURE, BUILDING, etc.

Construction.

THE SCIENCE OF BUILDING : *An Elementary Treatise on the Principles of Construction.* By E. WYNDHAM TARN, M.A., Architect. Second Edition, Revised, with 58 Engravings. Crown 8vo, 7s. 6d. cloth.

"A very valuable book, which we strongly recommend to all students."—*Builder.*

"No architectural student should be without this handbook of constructional knowledge."—*Architect.*

Villa Architecture.

A HANDY BOOK OF VILLA ARCHITECTURE : *Being a Series of Designs for Villa Residences in various Styles.* With Outline Specifications and Estimates. By C. WICKES, Architect, Author of " The Spires and Towers of England," &c. 61 Plates, 4to, £1 11s. 6d. half-morocco, gilt edges.

"The whole of the designs bear evidence of their being the work of an artistic architect, and they will prove very valuable and suggestive."—*Building News.*

Text-Book for Architects.

THE ARCHITECT'S GUIDE: *Being a Text-Book of Useful Information for Architects, Engineers, Surveyors, Contractors, Clerks of Works, &c. &c.* By FREDERICK ROGERS, Architect, Author of " Specifications for Practical Architecture," &c. Second Edition, Revised and Enlarged. With numerous Illustrations. Crown 8vo, 6s. cloth.

"As a text-book of useful information for architects, engineers, surveyors, &c., it would be hard to find a handier or more complete little volume."—*Standard.*

"A young architect could hardly have a better guide-book."—*Timber Trades Journal.*

Taylor and Cresy's Rome.

THE ARCHITECTURAL ANTIQUITIES OF ROME. By the late G. L. TAYLOR, Esq., F.R.I.B.A., and EDWARD CRESY, Esq. New Edition, thoroughly Revised by the Rev. ALEXANDER TAYLOR, M.A. (son of the late G. L. Taylor, Esq.), Fellow of Queen's College, Oxford, and Chaplain of Gray's Inn. Large folio, with 130 Plates, half-bound, £3 3s.

N.B.—*This is the only book which gives on a large scale, and with the precision of architectural measurement, the principal Monuments of Ancient Rome in plan, elevation, and detail.*

"Taylor and Cresy's work has from its first publication been ranked among those professional books which cannot be bettered. . . . It would be difficult to find examples of drawings, even among those of the most painstaking students of Gothic, more thoroughly worked out than are the one hundred and thirty plates in this volume."—*Architect.*

Architectural Drawing.

PRACTICAL RULES ON DRAWING, *for the Operative Builder and Young Student in Architecture.* By GEORGE PYNE. With 14 Plates, 4to. 7s. 6d. boards.

Civil Architecture.

THE DECORATIVE PART OF CIVIL ARCHITECTURE. By Sir WILLIAM CHAMBERS, F.R.S. With Illustrations, Notes, and an Examination of Grecian Architecture, by JOSEPH GWILT, F.S.A. Edited by W. H. LEEDS. 66 Plates, 4to, 21s. cloth.

House Building and Repairing.

THE HOUSE-OWNER'S ESTIMATOR ; or, What will it Cost to Build, Alter, or Repair? A Price Book adapted to the Use of Unprofessional People, as well as for the Architectural Surveyor and Builder. By JAMES D. SIMON, A.R.I.B.A. Edited and Revised by FRANCIS T. W. MILLER, A.R.I.B.A. With numerous Illustrations. Fourth Edition, Revised. Crown 8vo, 3s. 6d. cloth.   [*Just published.*

"In two years it will repay its cost a hundred times over"—*Field.*

"A very handy book."—*English Mechanic.*

Designing, Measuring, and Valuing.

THE STUDENT'S GUIDE to the PRACTICE of MEASUR-
ING AND VALUING ARTIFICERS' WORKS. Containing Directions for
taking Dimensions, Abstracting the same, and bringing the Quantities into
Bill, with Tables of Constants for Valuation of Labour, and for the Calcula-
tion of Areas and Solidities. Originally edited by EDWARD DOBSON, Architect.
Revised, with considerable Additions on Mensuration and Construction, and
a New Chapter on Dilapidations, Repairs, and Contracts, by E. WYNDHAM
TARN, M.A. Sixth Edition, including a Complete Form of a Bill of Quantities.
With 8 Plates and 63 Woodcuts.   Crown 8vo, 7s. 6d. cloth.   [Just published.

"Well fulfils the promise of its title-page, and we can thoroughly recommend it to the class
for whose use it has been compiled. Mr. Tarn's additions and revisions have much increased the
usefulness of the work, and have especially augmented its value to students."—Engineering.
"This edition will be found the most complete treatise on the principles of measuring and
valuing artificers' work that has yet been published."—Building News.

Pocket Estimator and Technical Guide.

THE POCKET TECHNICAL GUIDE, MEASURER AND
ESTIMATOR FOR BUILDERS AND SURVEYORS. Containing Technical Directions for Measuring Work in all the Building Trades, with a
Treatise on the Measurement of Timber and Complete Specifications for
Houses, Roads, and Drains, and an easy Method of Estimating the various
parts of a Building collectively. By A. C. BEATON, Author of "Quantities
and Measurements," &c.   Fifth Edition, carefully Revised and Priced
according to the Present Value of Materials and Labour, with 53 Woodcuts,
leather, waistcoat-pocket size, 1s. 6d. gilt edges.   [Just published.

"No builder, architect, surveyor, or valuer should be without his 'Beaton.''—Building News.
"Contains an extraordinary amount of information in daily requisition in measuring and
estimating. Its presence in the pocket will save valuable time and trouble."—Building World.

Donaldson on Specifications.

THE HANDBOOK OF SPECIFICATIONS; or, Practical
Guide to the Architect, Engineer, Surveyor, and Builder, in drawing up
Specifications and Contracts for Works and Constructions. Illustrated by
Precedents of Buildings actually executed by eminent Architects and En-
gineers. By Professor T. L. DONALDSON, P.R.I.B.A., &c.   New Edition, in
One large Vol., 8vo, with upwards of 1,000 pages of Text, and 33 Plates,
£1 11s. 6d. cloth.

"In this work forty-four specifications of executed works are given, including the specifications for parts of the new Houses of Parliament, by Sir Charles Barry, and for the new Royal
Exchange, by Mr. Tite, M.P. The latter, in particular, is a very complete and remarkable
document. It embodies, to a great extent, as Mr. Donaldson mentions, 'the bill of quantities
with the description of the works.' . . . It is valuable as a record, and more valuable still as a
book of precedents. . . . Suffice it to say that Donaldson's 'Handbook of Specifications'
must be bought by all architects."—Builder.

Bartholomew and Rogers' Specifications.

SPECIFICATIONS FOR PRACTICAL ARCHITECTURE.
A Guide to the Architect, Engineer, Surveyor, and Builder. With an Essay
on the Structure and Science of Modern Buildings.   Upon the Basis of the
Work by ALFRED BARTHOLOMEW, thoroughly Revised, Corrected, and greatly
added to by FREDERICK ROGERS, Architect.   Second Edition, Revised, with
Additions.   With numerous Illustrations, medium 8vo, 15s. cloth.

"The collection of specifications prepared by Mr. Rogers on the basis of Bartholomew's work
is too well known to need any recommendation from us. It is one of the books with which every
young architect must be equipped ; for time has shown that the specifications cannot be set aside
through any defect in them."—Architect.
"Good forms for specifications are of considerable value, and it was an excellent idea to com-
pile a work on the subject upon the basis of the late Alfred Bartholomew's valuable work. The
second edition of Mr. Rogers's book is evidence of the want of a book dealing with modern requirements and materials."—Building News.

Building ; Civil and Ecclesiastical.

A BOOK ON BUILDING, Civil and Ecclesiastical, including
Church Restoration ; with the Theory of Domes and the Great Pyramid, &c.
By Sir EDMUND BECKETT, Bart., LL.D., F.R.A.S., Author of "Clocks and
Watches, and Bells," &c.   Second Edition, Enlarged.   Fcap. 8vo, 5s. cloth.

"A book which is always amusing and nearly always instructive. The style throughout is in
the highest degree condensed and epigrammatic."—Times.

Geometry for the Architect, Engineer, etc.

PRACTICAL GEOMETRY, *for the Architect, Engineer and Mechanic.* Giving Rules for the Delineation and Application of various Geometrical Lines, Figures and Curves. By E. W. TARN, M.A., Architect, Author of "The Science of Building," &c. Second Edition. With Appendices on Diagrams of Strains and Isometrical Projection. With 172 Illustrations, demy 8vo, 9s. cloth.

"No book with the same objects in view has ever been published in which the clearness of the rules laid down and the illustrative diagrams have been so satisfactory."—*Scotsman.*
"This is a manual for the practical man, whether architect, engineer, or mechanic. . . . The object of the author being to avoid all abstruse formulæ or complicated methods, and to enable persons with but a moderate knowledge of geometry to work out the problems required."—*English Mechanic.*

The Science of Geometry.

THE GEOMETRY OF COMPASSES; *or, Problems Resolved by the mere Description of Circles, and the use of Coloured Diagrams and Symbols.* By OLIVER BYRNE. Coloured Plates. Crown 8vo, 3s. 6d. cloth.

"The treatise is a good one, and remarkable—like all Mr. Byrne's contributions to the science of geometry—for the lucid character of its teaching."—*Building News.*

DECORATIVE ARTS, etc.

Woods and Marbles (Imitation of).

SCHOOL OF PAINTING FOR THE IMITATION OF WOODS AND MARBLES, as Taught and Practised by A. R. VAN DER BURG and P. VAN DER BURG, Directors of the Rotterdam Painting Institution. Royal folio, 18½ by 12¼ in., Illustrated with 24 full-size Coloured Plates; also 12 plain Plates, comprising 154 Figures. Second and Cheaper Edition. Price £1 11s. 6d.

List of Plates.

1. Various Tools required for Wood Painting—2, 3. Walnut: Preliminary Stages of Graining and Finished Specimen—4. Tools used for Marble Painting and Method of Manipulation—5, 6. St. Remi Marble: Earlier Operations and Finished Specimen—7. Methods of Sketching different Grains, Knots, &c.—8, 9. Ash: Preliminary Stages and Finished Specimen—10. Methods of Sketching Marble Grains—11, 12. Breche Marble: Preliminary Stages of Working and Finished Specimen—13. Maple: Methods of Producing the different Grains—14, 15. Bird's-eye Maple: Preliminary Stages and Finished Specimen—16. Methods of Sketching the different Species of White Marble—17, 18. White Marble: Preliminary Stages of Process and Finished Specimen—19. Mahogany: Specimens of various Grains and Methods of Manipulation—20, 21. Mahogany: Earlier Stages and Finished Specimen—22, 23, 24. Sienna Marble: Varieties of Grain, Preliminary Stages and Finished Specimen—25, 26, 27. Juniper Wood: Methods of producing Grain, &c.: Preliminary Stages and Finished Specimen—28, 29, 30. Vert de Mer Marble: Varieties of Grain and Methods of Working Unfinished and Finished Specimens—31, 32, 33. Oak: Varieties of Grain, Tools Employed, and Methods of Manipulation, Preliminary Stages and Finished Specimen—34, 35, 36. Waulsort Marble: Varieties of Grain, Unfinished and Finished Specimens.

*** OPINIONS OF THE PRESS.

"Those who desire to attain skill in the art of painting woods and marbles will find advantage in consulting this book. . . . Some of the Working Men's Clubs should give their young men the opportunity to study it."—*Builder.*
"A comprehensive guide to the art. The explanations of the processes, the manipulation and management of the colours, and the beautifully executed plates will not be the least valuable to the student who aims at making his work a faithful transcript of nature."—*Building News.*
"Students and novices are fortunate who are able to become the possessors of *so noble a work.*"—*Architect.*

House Decoration.

ELEMENTARY DECORATION. A Guide to the Simpler Forms of Everyday Art, as applied to the Interior and Exterior Decoration of Dwelling Houses, &c. By JAMES W. FACEY, Jun. With 68 Cuts. 12mo, 2s. cloth limp.

'As a technical guide-book to the decorative painter it will be found reliable."—*Building News.*

PRACTICAL HOUSE DECORATION : A Guide to the Art of Ornamental Painting, the Arrangement of Colours in Apartments, and the principles of Decorative Design. With some Remarks upon the Nature and Properties of Pigments. By JAMES WILLIAM FACEY, Author of "Elementary Decoration," &c. With numerous Illustrations. 12mo, 2s. 6d. cloth limp.

N.B.—The above Two Works together in One Vol., strongly half-bound, 5s.

Colour.

A GRAMMAR OF COLOURING. Applied to Decorative Painting and the Arts. By GEORGE FIELD. New Edition, Revised, Enlarged, and adapted to the use of the Ornamental Painter and Designer. By ELLIS A. DAVIDSON. With New Coloured Diagrams and Engravings. 12mo, 3s. 6d. cloth boards.

" The book is a most useful *resume* of the properties of pigments."—*Builder.*

House Painting, Graining, etc.

HOUSE PAINTING, GRAINING, MARBLING, AND SIGN WRITING, A Practical Manual of. By ELLIS A. DAVIDSON. Fifth Edition. With Coloured Plates and Wood Engravings. 12mo, 6s. cloth boards.

" A mass of information, of use to the amateur and of value to the practical man."—*English Mechanic.*

"Simply invaluable to the youngster entering upon this particular calling, and highly serviceable to the man who is practising it."—*Furniture Gazette.*

Decorators, Receipts for.

THE DECORATOR'S ASSISTANT : A Modern Guide to Decorative Artists and Amateurs, Painters, Writers, Gilders, &c. Containing upwards of 600 Receipts, Rules and Instructions ; with a variety of Information for General Work connected with every Class of Interior and Exterior Decorations, &c. Third Edition, Revised. 152 pp., crown 8vo, 1s. in wrapper.

" Full of receipts of value to decorators, painters, gilders, &c. The book contains the gist of larger treatises on colour and technical processes. It would be difficult to meet with a work so full of varied information on the painter's art."—*Building News.*

" We recommend the work to all who, whether for pleasure or profit, require a guide to decoration."—*Plumber and Decorator.*

Moyr Smith on Interior Decoration.

ORNAMENTAL INTERIORS, ANCIENT AND MODERN. By J. MOYR SMITH. Super-royal 8vo, with 32 full-page Plates and numerous smaller Illustrations, handsomely bound in cloth, gilt top, price 18s.

☞ *In* "ORNAMENTAL INTERIORS" *the designs of more than thirty artist-decorators and architects of high standing have been illustrated. The book may therefore fairly claim to give a good general view of the works of the modern school of decoration, besides giving characteristic examples of earlier decorative arrangements.*

"ORNAMENTAL INTERIORS" *gives a short account of the styles of Interior Decoration as practised by the Ancients in Egypt, Greece, Assyria, Rome and Byzantium. This part is illustrated by characteristic designs.*

*** OPINIONS OF THE PRESS.

" The book is well illustrated and handsomely got up, and contains some true criticism and a good many good examples of decorative treatment."—*The Builder.*

" Well fitted for the dilettante, amateur, and professional designer."—*Decoration.*

" This is the most elaborate, and beautiful work on the artistic decoration of interiors that we have seen. . . . The scrolls, panels and other designs from the author's own pen are very beautiful and chaste ; but he takes care that the designs of other men shall figure even more than his own."—*Liverpool Albion.*

" To all who take an interest in elaborate domestic ornament this handsome volume will be welcome."—*Graphic.*

" Mr. Moyr Smith deserves the thanks of art workers for having placed within their reach a book that seems eminently adapted to afford, by example and precept, that guidance of which most craftsmen stand in need."—*Furniture Gazette.*

British and Foreign Marbles.

MARBLE DECORATION and the Terminology of British and Foreign Marbles. A Handbook for Students. By GEORGE H. BLAGROVE, Author of " Shoring and its Application," &c. With 28 Illustrations. Crown 8vo, 3s. 6d. cloth.

" This most useful and much wanted handbook should be in the hands of every architect and builder."—*Building World.*

" It is an excellent manual for students, and interesting to artistic readers generally."—*Saturday Review.*

" A carefully and usefully written eatise ; the work is essentially practical."—*Scotsman.*

Marble Working, etc.

MARBLE AND MARBLE WORKERS : A Handbook for Architects, Artists, Masons and Students. By ARTHUR LEE, Author of " A Visit to Carrara," " The Working of Marble," &c. Small crown 8vo, 2s. cloth.

" A really valuable addition to the technical literature of architects and masons."—*Building News.*

DELAMOTTE'S WORKS ON ILLUMINATION AND ALPHABETS.

A PRIMER OF THE ART OF ILLUMINATION, for the Use of
Beginners : with a Rudimentary Treatise on the Art, Practical Directions for
its exercise, and Examples taken from Illuminated MSS., printed in Gold and
Colours. By F. DELAMOTTE. New and Cheaper Edition. Small 4to, 6s. ornamental boards.

"The examples of ancient MSS. recommended to the student, which, with much good sense,
the author chooses from collections accessible to all, are selected with judgment and knowledge,
as well as taste."—*Athenæum.*

ORNAMENTAL ALPHABETS, Ancient and Mediæval, from the
Eighth Century, with Numerals; including Gothic, Church-Text, large and
small, German, Italian, Arabesque, Initials for Illumination, Monograms,
Crosses, &c. &c., for the use of Architectural and Engineering Draughtsmen,
Missal Painters, Masons, Decorative Painters, Lithographers, Engravers,
Carvers, &c. &c. Collected and Engraved by F. DELAMOTTE, and printed in
Colours. New and Cheaper Edition. Royal 8vo, oblong, 2s. 6d. ornamental
boards.

"For those who insert enamelled sentences round gilded chalices, who blazon shop legends over
shop-doors, who letter church walls with pithy sentences from the Decalogue, this book will be useful."—*Athenæum.*

EXAMPLES OF MODERN ALPHABETS, Plain and Ornamental ;
including German, Old English, Saxon, Italic, Perspective, Greek, Hebrew,
Court Hand; Engrossing, Tuscan, Riband, Gothic, Rustic, and Arabesque;
with several Original Designs, and an Analysis of the Roman and Old English
Alphabets, large and small, and Numerals, for the use of Draughtsmen, Surveyors, Masons, Decorative Painters, Lithographers, Engravers, Carvers, &c.
Collected and Engraved by F. DELAMOTTE, and printed in Colours. New
and Cheaper Edition. Royal 8vo, oblong, 2s. 6d. ornamental boards.

"There is comprised in it every possible shape into which the letters of the alphabet and
numerals can be formed, and the talent which has been expended in the conception of the various
plain and ornamental letters is wonderful."—*Standard.*

MEDIÆVAL ALPHABETS AND INITIALS FOR ILLUMI-
NATORS. By G. DELAMOTTE. Containing 21 Plates and Illuminated
Title, printed in Gold and Colours. With an Introduction by J. WILLIS
BROOKS. Fourth and Cheaper Edition. Small 4to, 4s. ornamental boards.

" A volume in which the letters of the alphabet come forth glorified in gilding and all the colours
of the prism interwoven and intertwined and intermingled."—*Sun.*

THE EMBROIDERER'S BOOK OF DESIGN. Containing
Initials, Emblems, Cyphers, Monograms, Ornamental Borders, Ecclesiastical
Devices, Mediæval and Modern Alphabets, and National Emblems. Collected by F. DELAMOTTE, and printed in Colours. Oblong royal 8vo, 1s. 6d.
ornamental wrapper.

"The book will be of great assistance to ladies and young children who are endowed with the
art of plying the needle in this most ornamental and useful pretty work."—*East Anglian Times.*

Wood Carving.

INSTRUCTIONS IN WOOD-CARVING, for Amateurs ; with
Hints on Design. By A LADY. With Ten large Plates, 2s. 6d. in emblematic
wrapper.

"The handicraft of the wood-carver, so well as a book can impart it, may be learnt from ' A
Lady's' publication."—*Athenæum.*
" The directions given are plain and easily understood."—*English Mechanic.*

Glass Painting.

GLASS STAINING AND THE ART OF PAINTING ON
GLASS. From the German of Dr. GESSERT and EMANUEL OTTO FROMBERG.
With an Appendix on THE ART OF ENAMELLING. 12mo, 2s. 6d. cloth limp.

Letter Painting.

THE ART OF LETTER PAINTING MADE EASY. By
JAMES GREIG BADENOCH. With 12 full-page Engravings of Examples, 1s. 6d.
cloth limp.

"The system is a simple one, but quite original, and well worth the careful attention of lett r
painters. It can be easily mastered and remembered."—*Building News.*

CARPENTRY, TIMBER, etc.

Tredgold's Carpentry, Enlarged by Tarn.

THE ELEMENTARY PRINCIPLES OF CARPENTRY.
A Treatise on the Pressure and Equilibrium of Timber Framing, the Resistance of Timber, and the Construction of Floors, Arches, Bridges, Roofs, Uniting Iron and Stone with Timber, &c. To which is added an Essay on the Nature and Properties of Timber, &c., with Descriptions of the kinds of Wood used in Building; also numerous Tables of the Scantlings of Timber for different purposes, the Specific Gravities of Materials, &c. By THOMAS TREDGOLD, C.E. With an Appendix of Specimens of Various Roofs of Iron and Stone, Illustrated. Seventh Edition, thoroughly revised and considerably enlarged by E. WYNDHAM TARN, M.A., Author of "The Science of Building," &c. With 61 Plates, Portrait of the Author, and several Woodcuts. In one large vol., 4to, price £1 5s. cloth.
"Ought to be in every architect's and every builder's library."—*Builder.*
"A work whose monumental excellence must commend it wherever skilful carpentry is concerned. The author's principles are rather confirmed than impaired by time. The additional plates are of great intrinsic value."—*Building News.*

Woodworking Machinery.

WOODWORKING MACHINERY : Its Rise, Progress, and Construction. With Hints on the Management of Saw Mills and the Economical Conversion of Timber. Illustrated with Examples of Recent Designs by leading English, French, and American Engineers. By M. POWIS BALE, A.M.Inst.C.E., M.I.M.E. Large crown 8vo, 12s. 6d. cloth.
"Mr. Bale is evidently an expert on the subject and he has collected so much information that his book is all-sufficient for builders and others engaged in the conversion of timber."—*Architect.*
"The most comprehensive compendium of wood-working machinery we have seen. The author is a thorough master of his subject."—*Building News.*
"The appearance of this book at the present time will, we should think, give a considerable impetus to the onward march of the machinist engaged in the designing and manufacture of wood-working machines. It should be in the office of every wood-working factory."—*English Mechanic.*

Saw Mills.

SAW MILLS : Their Arrangement and Management, and the Economical Conversion of Timber. (A Companion Volume to "Woodworking Machinery.") By M. POWIS BALE. With numerous Illustrations. Crown 8vo, 10s. 6d. cloth.
"The *administration* of a large sawing establishment is discussed, and the subject examined from a financial standpoint. Hence the size, shape, order, and disposition of saw-mills and the like are gone into in detail, and the course of the timber is traced from its reception to its delivery in its converted state. We could not desire a more complete or practical treatise."—*Builder.*
"We highly recommend Mr. Bale's work to the attention and perusal of all those who are engaged in the art of wood conversion, or who are about building or remodelling saw-mills on improved principles."—*Building News.*

Carpentering.

THE CARPENTER'S NEW GUIDE ; or, Book of Lines for Carpenters; comprising all the Elementary Principles essential for acquiring a knowledge of Carpentry. Founded on the late PETER NICHOLSON'S Standard Work. A New Edition, Revised by ARTHUR ASHPITEL, F.S.A. Together with Practical Rules on Drawing, by GEORGE PYNE. With 74 Plates, 4to, £1 1s. cloth.

Handrailing.

A PRACTICAL TREATISE ON HANDRAILING : Showing New and Simple Methods for Finding the Pitch of the Plank, Drawing the Moulds, Bevelling, Jointing-up, and Squaring the Wreath. By GEORGE COLLINGS. Illustrated with Plates and Diagrams. 12mo, 1s. 6d. cloth limp.
"Will be found of practical utility in the execution of this difficult branch of joinery."—*Builder.*
"Almost every difficult phase of this somewhat intricate branch of joinery is elucidated by the aid of plates and explanatory letterpress."—*Furniture Gazette.*

Circular Work.

CIRCULAR WORK IN CARPENTRY AND JOINERY : A Practical Treatise on Circular Work of Single and Double Curvature. By GEORGE COLLINGS, Author of "A Practical Treatise on Handrailing." Illustrated with numerous Diagrams. 12mo, 2s. 6d. cloth limp.
"An excellent example of what a book of this kind should be. Cheap in price, clear in definition and practical in the examples selected."—*Builder.*

Timber Merchant's Companion.

THE TIMBER MERCHANT'S AND BUILDER'S COM-PANION. Containing New and Copious Tables of the Reduced Weight and Measurement of Deals and Battens, of all sizes, from One to a Thousand Pieces, and the relative Price that each size bears per Lineal Foot to any given Price per Petersburg Standard Hundred; the Price per Cube Foot of Square Timber to any given Price per Load of 50 Feet; the proportionate Value of Deals and Battens by the Standard, to Square Timber by the Load of 50 Feet; the readiest mode of ascertaining the Price of Scantling per Lineal Foot of any size, to any given Figure per Cube Foot, &c. &c. By WILLIAM DOWSING. Fourth Edition, Revised and Corrected. Cr. 8vo, 3s. cl.

"Everything is as concise and clear as it can possibly be made. There can be no doubt that every timber merchant and builder ought to possess it."—*Hull Advertiser.*
"We are glad to see a fourth edition of these admirable tables, which for correctness and simplicity of arrangement leave nothing to be desired."—*Timber Trades Journal.*
"An exceedingly well-arranged, clear, and concise manual of tables for the use of all who buy or sell timber."—*Journal of Forestry.*

Practical Timber Merchant.

THE PRACTICAL TIMBER MERCHANT. Being a Guide for the use of Building Contractors, Surveyors, Builders, &c., comprising useful Tables for all purposes connected with the Timber Trade, Marks of Wood, Essay on the Strength of Timber, Remarks on the Growth of Timber, &c. By W. RICHARDSON. Fcap. 8vo, 3s. 6d. cloth.

"Contains much valuable information for the use of timber merchants, builders, foresters, and all others connected with the growth, sale, and manufacture of timber.'—*Journal of Forestry.*

Timber Freight Book.

THE TIMBER MERCHANT'S, SAW MILLER'S, AND IMPORTER'S FREIGHT BOOK AND ASSISTANT. Comprising Rules, Tables, and Memoranda relating to the Timber Trade. By WILLIAM RICHARDSON, Timber Broker; together with a Chapter on "SPEEDS OF SAW MILL MACHINERY," by M. POWIS BALE, M.I.M.E., &c., 12mo, 3s. 6d. cl. boards.

"A very useful manual of rules, tables, and memoranda relating to the timber trade. We recommend it as a compendium of calculation to all timber measurers and merchants, and as supplying a real want in the trade."—*Building News.*

Packing-Case Makers, Tables for.

PACKING-CASE TABLES; showing the number of Superficial Feet in Boxes or Packing-Cases, from six inches square and upwards. By W. RICHARDSON, Timber Broker. Second Edition. Oblong 4to, 3s. 6d. cl

"Invaluable labour-saving tables."—*Ironmonger.*
"Will save much labour and calculation."—*Grocer.*

Superficial Measurement.

THE TRADESMAN'S GUIDE TO SUPERFICIAL MEASUREMENT. Tables calculated from 1 to 200 inches in length, by 1 to 108 inches in breadth. For the use of Architects, Surveyors, Engineers, Timber Merchants, Builders, &c. By JAMES HAWKINGS. Third Edition. Fcap., 3s. 6d. cloth.

"A useful collection of tables to facilitate rapid calculation of surfaces. The exact area of any surface of which the limits have been ascertained can be instantly determined. The book will be found of the greatest utility to all engaged in building operations."—*Scotsman.*
"These tables will be found of great assistance to all who require to make calculations in superficial measurement."—*English Mechanic.*

Forestry.

THE ELEMENTS OF FORESTRY. Designed to afford Information concerning the Planting and Care of Forest Trees for Ornament or Profit, with Suggestions upon the Creation and Care of Woodlands. By F. B. HOUGH. Large crown 8vo, 10s. cloth.

Timber Importer's Guide.

THE TIMBER IMPORTER'S, TIMBER MERCHANT'S AND BUILDER'S STANDARD GUIDE. By RICHARD E. GRANDY. Comprising an Analysis of Deal Standards, Home and Foreign, with Comparative Values and Tabular Arrangements for fixing Nett Landed Cost on Baltic and North American Deals, including all intermediate Expenses, Freight, Insurance, &c. &c. Together with copious Information for the Retailer and Builder. Third Edition, Revised. 12mo, 2s. cloth limp.

"Everything it pretends to be: built up gradually, it leads one from a forest to a treenall, and throws in, as a makeweight, a host of material concerning bricks, columns, cisterns, &c."—*English Mechanic.*

MARINE ENGINEERING, NAVIGATION, etc.

Chain Cables.

CHAIN CABLES AND CHAINS. Comprising Sizes and Curves of Links, Studs, &c., Iron for Cables and Chains, Chain Cable and Chain Making, Forming and Welding Links, Strength of Cables and Chains, Certificates for Cables, Marking Cables, Prices of Chain Cables and Chains, Historical Notes, Acts of Parliament, Statutory Tests, Charges for Testing, List of Manufacturers of Cables, &c. &c. By THOMAS W. TRAILL, F.E.R.N., M. Inst. C.E., Engineer Surveyor in Chief, Board of Trade, Inspector of Chain Cable and Anchor Proving Establishments, and General Superintendent, Lloyd's Committee on Proving Establishments. With numerous Tables, Illustrations and Lithographic Drawings. Folio, £2 2s. cloth.
"It contains a vast amount of valuable information. Nothing seems to be wanting to make it a complete and standard work of reference on the subject."—*Nautical Magazine.*

Marine Engineering.

MARINE ENGINES AND STEAM VESSELS (A Treatise on). By ROBERT MURRAY, C.E. Eighth Edition, thoroughly Revised, with considerable Additions by the Author and by GEORGE CARLISLE, C.E., Senior Surveyor to the Board of Trade at Liverpool. 12mo, 5s. cloth boards.
"Well adapted to give the young steamship engineer or marine engine and boiler maker a general introduction into his practical work."—*Mechanical World.*
"We feel sure that this thoroughly revised edition will continue to be as popular in the future as it has been in the past, as for its size, it contains more useful information than any similar treatise."—*Industries.*
"The information given is both sound and sensible, and well qualified to direct young seagoing hands on the straight road to the extra chief's certificate."—*Glasgow Herald.*
"An indispensable manual for the student of marine engineering."—*Liverpool Mercury.*

Pocket-Book for Naval Architects and Shipbuilders.

THE NAVAL ARCHITECT'S AND SHIPBUILDER'S POCKET-BOOK of Formulæ, Rules, and Tables, and MARINE ENGINEER'S AND SURVEYOR'S Handy Book of Reference. By CLEMENT MACKROW, Member of the Institution of Naval Architects, Naval Draughtsman. Third Edition, Revised. With numerous Diagrams, &c. Fcap., 12s. 6d. leather.
"Should be used by all who are engaged in the construction or design of vessels. . . . Will be found to contain the most useful tables and formulæ required by shipbuilders, carefully collected from the best authorities, and put together in a popular and simple form."—*Engineer.*
"The professional shipbuilder has now, in a convenient and accessible form, reliable data for solving many of the numerous problems that present themselves in the course of his work."—*Iron.*
"There is scarcely a subject on which a naval architect or shipbuilder can require to refresh his memory which will not be found within the covers of Mr. Mackrow's book."—*English Mechanic.*

Pocket-Book for Marine Engineers.

A POCKET-BOOK OF USEFUL TABLES AND FORMULÆ FOR MARINE ENGINEERS. By FRANK PROCTOR, A.I.N.A. Third Edition. Royal 32mo, leather, gilt edges, with strap, 4s.
"We recommend it to our readers as going far to supply a long-felt want."—*Naval Science.*
"A most useful companion to all marine engineers."—*United Service Gazette.*

Introduction to Marine Engineering.

ELEMENTARY ENGINEERING : A Manual for Young Marine Engineers and Apprentices. In the Form of Questions and Answers on Metals, Alloys, Strength of Materials, Construction and Management of Marine Engines, &c. &c. With an Appendix of Useful Tables. By J. S. BREWER, Government Marine Surveyor, Hongkong. Small crown 8vo, 2s. 6d. cloth. [*Just published*
"Contains much valuable information for the class for whom it is intended, especially in the chapters on the management of boilers and engines."—*Nautical Magazine.*
"A useful introduction to the more elaborate text books."—*Scotsman.*
"To a student who has the requisite desire and resolve to attain a thorough knowledge, Mr Brewer offers decidedly useful help."—*Athenæum.*

Navigation.

PRACTICAL NAVIGATION. Consisting of THE SAILOR'S SEA-BOOK, by JAMES GREENWOOD and W. H. ROSSER; together with the requisite Mathematical and Nautical Tables for the Working of the Problems. By HENRY LAW, C.E., and Professor J. R. YOUNG. Illustrated. 12mo, 7s. strongly half-bound.

MINING AND MINING INDUSTRIES.

Metalliferous Mining.

BRITISH MINING: *A Treatise on the History, Discovery, Practical Development, and Future Prospects of Metalliferous Mines in the United Kingdom.* By ROBERT HUNT, F.R.S., Keeper of Mining Records; Editor of "Ure's Dictionary of Arts, Manufactures, and Mines," &c. Upwards of 950 pp., with 230 Illustrations. Second Edition, Revised. Super-royal 8vo, £2 2s. cloth.

"One of the most valuable works of reference of modern times. Mr. Hunt, as keeper of mining records of the United Kingdom, has had opportunities for such a task not enjoyed by anyone else, and has evidently made the most of them. . . . The language and style adopted are good, and the treatment of the various subjects laborious, conscientious, and scientific."—*Engineering.*

"The book is, in fact, a treasure-house of statistical information on mining subjects, and we know of no other work embodying so great a mass of matter of this kind. Were this the only merit of Mr. Hunt's volume, it would be sufficient to render it indispensable in the library of everyone interested in the development of the mining and metallurgical industries of the country."—*Athenæum.*

"A mass of information not elsewhere available, and of the greatest value to those who may be interested in our great mineral industries."—*Engineer.*

"A sound, business-like collection of interesting facts. . . . The amount of information Mr. Hunt has brought together is enormous. . . . The volume appears likely to convey more instruction upon the subject than any work hitherto published."—*Mining Journal.*

"The work will be for the mining industry what Dr. Percy's celebrated treatise has been for the metallurgical—a book that cannot with advantage be omitted from the library."—*Iron and Coal Trades Review.*

"The volume is massive and exhaustive, and the high intellectual powers and patient, persistent application which characterise the author have evidently been brought into play in its production. Its contents are invaluable."—*Colliery Guardian.*

Coal and Iron.

THE COAL AND IRON INDUSTRIES OF THE UNITED KINGDOM. Comprising a Description of the Coal Fields, with Returns of their Produce and its Distribution, and Analyses of Special Varieties. Also an Account of the occurrence of Iron Ores in Veins or Seams; Analyses of each Variety; and a History of the Rise and Progress of Pig Iron Manufacture since the year 1740. By RICHARD MEADE, Assistant Keeper of Mining Records. With Maps of the Coal Fields and Ironstone Deposits of the United Kingdom. 8vo, £1 8s. cloth.

"The book is one which must find a place on the shelves of all interested in coal and iron production, and in the iron, steel, and other metallurgical industries."—*Engineer.*

"Of this book we may unreservedly say that it is the best of its class which we have ever met. . . . A book of reference which no one engaged in the iron or coal trades should omit from his library."—*Iron and Coal Trades Review.*

"An exhaustive treatise and a valuable work of reference."—*Mining Journal.*

Prospecting for Gold and other Metals.

THE PROSPECTOR'S HANDBOOK: A Guide for the Prospector and Traveller in Search of Metal-Bearing or other Valuable Minerals. By J. W. ANDERSON, M.A. (Camb.), F.R.G.S., Author of "Fiji and New Caledonia." Fourth Edition, thoroughly Revised and Enlarged. Small crown 8vo, 3s. 6d. cloth.   [*Just published.*

"Will supply a much felt want, especially among Colonists, in whose way are so often thrown many mineralogical specimens the value of which it is difficult for anyone, not a specialist, to determine. The author has placed his instructions before his readers in the plainest possible terms, and his book is the best of its kind."—*Engineer.*

"How to find commercial minerals, and how to identify them when they are found, are the leading points to which attention is directed. The author has managed to pack as much practical detail into his pages as would supply material for a book three times its size."—*Mining Journal.*

"Those toilers who explore the trodden or untrodden tracks on the face of the globe will find much that is useful to them in this book."—*Athenæum.*

Mining Notes and Formulæ.

NOTES AND FORMULÆ FOR MINING STUDENTS. By JOHN HERMAN MERIVALE, M.A., Certificated Colliery Manager, Professor of Mining in the Durham College of Science, Newcastle-upon-Tyne. Second Edition, carefully Revised. Small crown 8vo, cloth, price 2s. 6d.

"Invaluable to anyone who is working up for an examination on mining subjects."—*Coal and Iron Trades Review.*

"The author has done his work in an exceedingly creditable manner, and has produced a book that will be of service to students, and those who are practically engaged in mining operations."—*Engineer.*

"A vast amount of technical matter of the utmost value to mining engineers, and of considerable interest to students."—*Schoolmaster*

Gold, Metallurgy of.

THE METALLURGY OF GOLD : A Practical Treatise on the *Metallurgical Treatment of Gold-bearing Ores.* Including the Processes of Concentration and Chlorination, and the Assaying, Melting and Refining of Gold. By M. EISSLER, Mining Engineer and Metallurgical Chemist, formerly Assistant Assayer of the U. S. Mint, San Francisco. Second Edition, Revised and much Enlarged. With 132 Illustrations. Crown 8vo, 9s. cloth.

[*Just published.*

" This book thoroughly deserves its title of a 'Practical Treatise.' The whole process of gold milling, from the breaking of the quartz to the assay of the bullion, is described in clear and orderly narrative and with much, but not too much, fulness of detail."—*Saturday Review.*

" The work is a storehouse of information and valuable data, and we strongly recommend it to all professional men engaged in the gold-mining industry."—*Mining Journal.*

" Anyone who wishes to have an intelligent acquaintance with the characteristics of gold and gold ores, the methods of extracting the metal, concentrating and chlorinating it, and further on of refining and assaying it, will find all he wants in Mr. Eissler's book."—*Financial News.*

Silver, Metallurgy of.

THE METALLURGY OF SILVER : A Practical Treatise on the *Amalgamation, Roasting and Lixiviation of Silver Ores.* Including the Assaying, Melting and Refining of Silver Bullion. By M. EISSLER, Author of " The Metallurgy of Gold." With 124 Illustrations. Crown 8vo, 10s. 6d. cloth.

[*Just published.*

" A practical treatise, and a technical work which we are convinced will supply a long-felt want amongst practical men, and at the same time be of value to students and others indirectly connected with the industries."—*Mining Journal.*

" From first to last the book is thoroughly sound and reliable."—*Colliery Guardian.*

" For chemists, practical miners, assayers and investors alike, we do not know of any work on the subject so handy and yet so comprehensive."—*Glasgow Herald.*

Mineral Surveying and Valuing.

THE MINERAL SURVEYOR AND VALUER'S COMPLETE GUIDE, comprising a Treatise on Improved Mining Surveying and the Valuation of Mining Properties, with New Traverse Tables. By WM. LINTERN, Mining and Civil Engineer. Third Edition, with an Appendix on " Magnetic and Angular Surveying," With Four Plates. 12mo, 4s. cloth.

" An enormous fund of information of great value."—*Mining Journal.*

" Mr. Lintern's book forms a valuable and thoroughly trustworthy guide."—*Iron and Coal Trades Review.*

" This new edition must be of the highest value to colliery surveyors, proprietors and managers."—*Colliery Guardian.*

Metalliferous Minerals and Mining.

TREATISE ON METALLIFEROUS MINERALS AND MINING. By D. C. DAVIES, F.G.S., Mining Engineer, &c., Author of " A Treatise on Slate and Slate Quarrying." Illustrated with numerous Wood Engravings. Fourth Edition, carefully Revised. Crown 8vo, 12s. 6d. cloth.

" Neither the practical miner nor the general reader interested in mines can have a better book or his companion and his guide."—*Mining Journal.*

" The volume is one which no student of mineralogy should be without."—*Colliery Guardian.*

" A book that will not only be useful to the geologist, the practical miner, and the metallurgist, but also very interesting to the general public."—*Iron.*

" As a history of the present state of mining throughout the world this book has a real value, and it supplies an actual want, for no such information has hitherto been brought together within such limited space."—*Athenæum.*

Earthy Minerals and Mining.

TREATISE ON EARTHY AND OTHER MINERALS AND MINING. By D. C. DAVIES, F.G.S. Uniform with, and forming a Companion Volume to, the same Author's " Metalliferous Minerals and Mining." With 76 Wood Engravings. Second Edition. Crown 8vo, 12s. 6d. cloth.

" It is essentially a practical work, intended primarily for the use of practical men. . . . We do not remember to have met with any English work on mining matters that contains the same amount of information packed in equally convenient form."—*Academy.*

" The book is clearly the result of many years' careful work and thought, and we should be inclined to rank it as among the very best of the handy technical and trades manuals which have recently appeared."—*British Quarterly Review.*

" The volume contains a great mass of practical information carefully methodised and presented in a very intelligible shape."—*Scotsman.*

" The subject matter of the volume will be found of high value by all—and they are a numerous class—who trade in earthy minerals."—*Athenæum.*

Underground Pumping Machinery.

MINE DRAINAGE. Being a Complete and Practical Treatise on Direct-Acting Underground Steam Pumping Machinery, with a Description of a large number of the best known Engines, their General Utility and the Special Sphere of their Action, the Mode of their Application, and their merits compared with other forms of Pumping Machinery. By STEPHEN MICHELL. 8vo, 15s. cloth.

"Will be highly esteemed by colliery owners and lessees, mining engineers, and students generally who require to be acquainted with the best means of securing the drainage of mines. It is a most valuable work, and stands almost alone in the literature of steam pumping machinery."—*Colliery Guardian.*
" Much valuable information is given, so that the book is thoroughly worthy of an extensive circulation amongst practical men and purchasers of machinery. '—*Mining Journal.*

Mining Tools.

A MANUAL OF MINING TOOLS. For the Use of Mine Managers, Agents, Students, &c. By WILLIAM MORGANS, Lecturer on Practical Mining at the Bristol School of Mines. 12mo, 2s. 6d. cloth limp.

ATLAS OF ENGRAVINGS to Illustrate the above, containing 235 Illustrations of Mining Tools, drawn to scale. 4to, 4s. 6d. cloth.

"Students in the science of mining, and overmen, captains, managers, and viewers may gain practical knowledge and useful hints by the study of Mr. Morgans' manual."—*Colliery Guardian.*
"A valuable work, which will tend materially to improve our mining literature."—*Mining Journal.*

Coal Mining.

COAL AND COAL MINING : A Rudimentary Treatise on. By Sir WARINGTON W. SMYTH, M.A., F.R.S., &c., Chief Inspector of the Mines of the Crown. New Edition, Revised and Corrected. With numerous Illustrations. 12mo, 4s. cloth boards.

"As an outline is given of every known coal-field in this and other countries, as well as of the principal methods of working, the book will doubtless interest a very large number of readers."—*Mining Journal.*

Granite Quarrying.

GRANITES AND OUR GRANITE INDUSTRIES. By GEORGE F. HARRIS, F.G.S., Membre de la Société Belge de Géologie, Lecturer on Economic Geology at the Birkbeck Institution, &c. With Illustrations. Crown 8vo, 2s. 6d. cloth.

" A clearly and well-written manual for persons engaged or interested in the granite industry."—*Scotsman.*
" An interesting work, which will be deservedly esteemed. We advise the author to write again."—*Colliery Guardian.*
" An exceedingly interesting and valuable monograph, on a subject which has hitherto received unaccountably little attention in the shape of systematic literary treatment."—*Scottish Leader.*

NATURAL AND APPLIED SCIENCE.

Text Book of Electricity.

THE STUDENT'S TEXT-BOOK OF ELECTRICITY. By HENRY M. NOAD, Ph.D., F.R.S., F.C.S. New Edition, carefully Revised. With an Introduction and Additional Chapters, by W. H. PREECE, M.I.C.E., Vice-President of the Society of Telegraph Engineers, &c. With 470 Illustrations. Crown 8vo, 12s. 6d. cloth.

" The original plan of this book has been carefully adhered to so as to make it a reflex of the existing state of electrical science, adapted for students. . . . Discovery seems to have progressed with marvellous strides ; nevertheless it has now apparently ceased, and practical applications have commenced their career ; and it is to give a faithful account of these that this fresh edition of Dr. Noad's valuable text-book is launched forth."—*Extract from Introduction by W. H. Preece, Esq.*
" We can recommend Dr. Noad's book for clear style, great range of subject, a good index and a plethora of woodcuts. Such collections as the present are indispensable."—*Athenæum.*
" An admirable text book for every student — beginner or advanced — of electricity."—*Engineering.*

Electricity.

A MANUAL OF ELECTRICITY : Including Galvanism, Magnetism, Dia-Magnetism, Electro-Dynamics, Magno-Electricity, and the Electric Telegraph. By HENRY M. NOAD, Ph.D., F.R.S., F.C.S. Fourth Edition With 500 Woodcuts. 8vo, £1 4s. cloth.

"It is worthy of a place in the library of every public institution."—*Mining Journal.*

Electric Light.

ELECTRIC LIGHT : *Its Production and Use.* Embodying Plain Directions for the Treatment of Voltaic Batteries, Electric Lamps, and Dynamo-Electric Machines. By J. W. URQUHART, C.E., Author of " Electro-plating : A Practical Handbook." Edited by F. C. WEBB, M.I.C.E., M.S.T.E. Second Edition, Revised, with large Additions and 128 Illusts. 7s. 6d. cloth.
" The book is by far the best that we have yet met with on the subject."—*Athenaum.*
" It is the only work at present available which gives, in language intelligible for the most part to the ordinary reader, a general but concise history of the means which have been adopted up to the present time in producing the electric light."—*Metropolitan.*
" The book contains a general account of the means adopted in producing the electric light, not only as obtained from voltaic or galvanic batteries, but treats at length of the dynamo-electric machine in several of its forms."—*Colliery Guardian.*

Electric Lighting.

THE ELEMENTARY PRINCIPLES OF ELECTRIC LIGHT-ING. By ALAN A. CAMPBELL SWINTON, Associate I.E.E. Second Edition, Enlarged and Revised. With 16 Illustrations. Crown 8vo, 1s. 6d. cloth.
" Anyone who desires a short and thoroughly clear exposition of the elementary principles of electric-lighting cannot do better than read this little work."—*Bradford Observer.*

Dr. Lardner's School Handbooks.

NATURAL PHILOSOPHY FOR SCHOOLS. By Dr. LARDNER. 328 Illustrations. Sixth Edition. One Vol., 3s. 6d. cloth.
" A very convenient class-book for junior students in private schools. It is intended to convey, in clear and precise terms, general notions of all the principal divisions of Physical Science."—*British Quarterly Review.*

ANIMAL PHYSIOLOGY FOR SCHOOLS. By Dr. LARDNER. With 190 Illustrations. Second Edition. One Vol., 3s. 6d. cloth.
" Clearly written, well arranged, and excellently illustrated."—*Gardener's Chronicle.*

Dr. Lardner's Electric Telegraph.

THE ELECTRIC TELEGRAPH. By Dr. LARDNER. Re-vised and Re-written by E. B. BRIGHT, F.R.A.S. 140 Illustrations. Small 8vo, 2s. 6d. cloth.
" One of the most readable books extant on the Electric Telegraph."—*English Mechanic.*

Astronomy.

ASTRONOMY. By the late Rev. ROBERT MAIN, M.A., F.R.S., formerly Radcliffe Observer at Oxford. Third Edition, Revised and Cor-rected to the present time, by WILLIAM THYNNE LYNN, B.A., F.R.A.S., formerly of the Royal Observatory, Greenwich. 12mo, 2s. cloth limp.
" A sound and simple treatise, very carefully edited, and a capital book for beginners."— *Knowledge.* [*tional Times.*
" Accurately brought down to the requirements of the present time by Mr. Lynn."—*Educa-*

The Blowpipe.

THE BLOWPIPE IN CHEMISTRY, MINERALOGY, AND GEOLOGY. Containing all known Methods of Anhydrous Analysis, many Working Examples, and Instructions for Making Apparatus. By Lieut.-Colonel W. A. ROSS, R.A., F.G.S. With 120 Illustrations. Second Edition, Revised and Enlarged. Crown 8vo, 5s. cloth. [*Just published.*
" The student who goes conscientiously through the course of experimentation here laid down will gain a better insight into inorganic chemistry and mineralogy than if he had 'got up' any of the best text-books of the day, and passed any number of examinations in their contents."—*Chemical News.*

The Military Sciences.

AIDE-MEMOIRE TO THE MILITARY SCIENCES. Framed from Contributions of Officers and others connected with the different Ser-vices. Originally edited by a Committee of the Corps of Royal Engineers. Second Edition, most carefully Revised by an Officer of the Corps, with many Additions; containing nearly 350 Engravings and many hundred Woodcuts. Three Vols., royal 8vo, extra cloth boards, and lettered, £4 10s.
" A compendious encyclopædia of military knowledge, to which we are greatly indebted."— *Edinburgh Review.*
" The most comprehensive book of reference to the military and collateral sciences."— *Volunteer Service Gazette.*

Field Fortification.

A TREATISE ON FIELD FORTIFICATION, THE ATTACK OF FORTRESSES, MILITARY MINING, AND RECONNOITRING. By Colonel I. S. MACAULAY, late Professor of Fortification in the R.M.A., Wool-wich. Sixth Edition, crown 8vo, cloth, with separate Atlas of 12 Plates, 12s.

Temperaments.

OUR TEMPERAMENTS, THEIR STUDY AND THEIR TEACHING. *A Popular Outline.* By ALEXANDER STEWART, F.R.C.S. Edin. In one large 8vo volume, with 30 Illustrations, including A Selection from Lodge's "Historical Portraits," showing the Chief Forms of Faces. Price 15s. cloth, gilt top.

"The book is exceedingly interesting, even for those who are not systematic students of anthropology. . . . To those who think the proper study of mankind is man, it will be full of attraction."—*Daily Telegraph.*

"The author's object is to enable a student to read a man's temperament in his aspect. The work is well adapted to its end. It is worthy of the attention of students of human nature."—*Scotsman.*

"The volume is heavy to hold, but light to read. Though the author has treated his subject exhaustively, he writes in a popular and pleasant manner that renders it attractive to the general reader."—*Punch.*

Antiseptic Nursing.

ANTISEPTICS: *A Handbook for Nurses.* Being an Epitome of Antiseptic Treatment. With Notes on Antiseptic Substances, Disinfection, Monthly Nursing, &c. By Mrs. ANNIE HEWER, late Hospital Sister, Diplomée Obs. Soc. Lond. Crown 8vo, 1s. 6d. cloth. [*Just published.*

"This excellent little work . . . is very readable and contains much information. We can strongly recommend it to those who are undergoing training at the various hospitals, and also to those who are engaged in the practice of nursing, as they cannot fail to obtain practical hints from its perusal."—*Lancet.*

"The student or the busy practitioner would do well to look through its pages, offering as they do a suggestive and faithful picture of antiseptic methods."—*Hospital Gazette.*

"A clear, concise, and excellent little handbook."—*The Hospital.*

Pneumatics and Acoustics.

PNEUMATICS: *including Acoustics and the Phenomena of Wind Currents,* for the Use of Beginners. By CHARLES TOMLINSON, F.R.S., F.C.S., &c. Fourth Edition, Enlarged. With numerous Illustrations. 12mo, 1s. 6d. cloth.

"Beginners in the study of this important application of science could not have a better manual."—*Scotsman.*

"A valuable and suitable text-book for students of Acoustics and the Phenomena of Wind Currents."—*Schoolmaster.*

Conchology.

A MANUAL OF THE MOLLUSCA: *Being a Treatise on Recent and Fossil Shells.* By S. P. WOODWARD, A.L.S., F.G.S., late Assistant Palæontologist in the British Museum. Fifth Edition. With an Appendix on *Recent and Fossil Conchological Discoveries,* by RALPH TATE, A.L.S., F.G.S. Illustrated by A. N. WATERHOUSE and JOSEPH WILSON LOWRY. With 23 Plates and upwards of 300 Woodcuts. Crown 8vo, 7s. 6d. cloth boards.

"A most valuable storehouse of conchological and geological information."—*Science Gossip.*

Geology.

RUDIMENTARY TREATISE ON GEOLOGY, PHYSICAL AND HISTORICAL. Consisting of "Physical Geology," which sets forth the leading Principles of the Science; and "Historical Geology," which treats of the Mineral and Organic Conditions of the Earth at each successive epoch, especial reference being made to the British Series of Rocks. By RALPH TATE, A.L.S., F.G.S., &c., &c. With 250 Illustrations. 12mo, 5s. cloth boards.

"The fulness of the matter has elevated the book into a manual. Its information is exhaustive and well arranged."—*School Board Chronicle.*

Geology and Genesis.

THE TWIN RECORDS OF CREATION; or, *Geology and Genesis: their Perfect Harmony and Wonderful Concord.* By GEORGE W. VICTOR LE VAUX. Numerous Illustrations. Fcap. 8vo, 5s. cloth.

"A valuable contribution to the evidences of Revelation, and disposes very conclusively of the arguments of those who would set God's Works against God's Word. No real difficulty is shirked, and no sophistry is left unexposed."—*The Rock.*

"The remarkable peculiarity of this author is that he combines an unbounded admiration of science with an unbounded admiration of the Written record. The two impulses are balanced to a nicety; and the consequence is that difficulties, which to minds less evenly poised would be serious, find immediate solutions of the happiest kinds."—*London Review.*

DR. LARDNER'S HANDBOOKS OF NATURAL PHILOSOPHY.

THE HANDBOOK OF MECHANICS. Enlarged and almost re-written by BENJAMIN LOEWY, F.R.A.S. With 378 Illustrations. Post 8vo, 6s. cloth.

"The perspicuity of the original has been retained, and chapters which had become obsolete have been replaced by others of more modern character. The explanations throughout are studiously popular, and care has been taken to show the application of the various branches of physics to the industrial arts, and to the practical business of life."—*Mining Journal.*

"Mr. Loewy has carefully revised the book, and brought it up to modern requirements."—*Nature.*

"Natural philosophy has had few exponents more able or better skilled in the art of popularising the subject than Dr. Lardner; and Mr. Loewy is doing good service in fitting this treatise, and the others of the series, for use at the present time."—*Scotsman.*

THE HANDBOOK OF HYDROSTATICS AND PNEUMATICS. New Edition, Revised and Enlarged, by BENJAMIN LOEWY, F.R.A.S. With 236 Illustrations. Post 8vo, 5s. cloth.

"For those 'who desire to attain an accurate knowledge of physical science without the profound methods of mathematical investigation,' this work is not merely intended, but well adapted."—*Chemical News.*

"The volume before us has been carefully edited, augmented to nearly twice the bulk of the former edition, and all the most recent matter has been added. . . . It is a valuable text-book."—*Nature.*

"Candidates for pass examinations will find it, we think, specially suited to their requirements. *English Mechanic.*

THE HANDBOOK OF HEAT. Edited and almost entirely re-written by BENJAMIN LOEWY, F.R.A.S., &c. 117 Illustrations. Post 8vo, 6s. cloth.

"The style is always clear and precise, and conveys instruction without leaving any cloudiness or lurking doubts behind."—*Engineering.*

"A most exhaustive book on the subject on which it treats, and is so arranged that it can be understood by all who desire to attain an accurate knowledge of physical science. . . . . Mr. Loewy has included all the latest discoveries in the varied laws and effects of heat."—*Standard.*

"A complete and handy text-book for the use of students and general readers."—*English Mechanic.*

THE HANDBOOK OF OPTICS. By DIONYSIUS LARDNER, D.C.L., formerly Professor of Natural Philosophy and Astronomy in University College, London. New Edition. Edited by T. OLVER HARDING, B.A. Lond., of University College, London. With 298 Illustrations. Small 8vo, 448 pages, 5s. cloth.

"Written by one of the ablest English scientific writers, beautifully and elaborately illustrated." *Mechanic's Magazine.*

THE HANDBOOK OF ELECTRICITY, MAGNETISM, AND ACOUSTICS. By Dr. LARDNER. Ninth Thousand. Edit. by GEORGE CAREY FOSTER, B.A., F.C.S. With 400 Illustrations. Small 8vo, 5s. cloth.

"The book could not have been entrusted to anyone better calculated to preserve the terse and lucid style of Lardner, while correcting his errors and bringing up his work to the present state of scientific knowledge."—*Popular Science Review.*

. *The above Five Volumes, though each is Complete in itself, form* A COMPLETE COURSE OF NATURAL PHILOSOPHY.

Dr. Lardner's Handbook of Astronomy.

THE HANDBOOK OF ASTRONOMY. Forming a Companion to the "Handbook of Natural Philosophy." By DIONYSIUS LARDNER, D.C.L., formerly Professor of Natural Philosophy and Astronomy in University College, London. Fourth Edition. Revised and Edited by EDWIN DUNKIN, F.R.A.S., Royal Observatory, Greenwich. With 38 Plates and upwards of 100 Woodcuts. In One Vol., small 8vo, 550 pages, 9s. 6d. cloth.

"Probably no other book contains the same amount of information in so compendious and well-arranged a form—certainly none at the price at which this is offered to the public."—*Athenæum.*

"We can do no other than pronounce this work a most valuable manual of astronomy, and we strongly recommend it to all who wish to acquire a general—but at the same time correct—acquaintance with this sublime science."—*Quarterly Journal of Science.*

"One of the most deservedly popular books on the subject . . . We would recommend not only the student of the elementary principles of the science, but he who aims at mastering the higher and mathematical branches of astronomy, not to be without this work beside him."—*Practical Magazine.*

DR. LARDNER'S MUSEUM OF SCIENCE AND ART.

THE MUSEUM OF SCIENCE AND ART. Edited by DIONYSIUS LARDNER, D.C.L., formerly Professor of Natural Philosophy and Astronomy in University College, London. With upwards of 1,200 Engravings on Wood. In 6 Double Volumes, £1 1s., in a new and elegant cloth binding; or handsomely bound in half-morocco, 31s. 6d.

Contents:

The Planets: Are they Inhabited Worlds?—Weather Prognostics — Popular Fallacies in Questions of Physical Science—Latitudes and Longitudes — Lunar Influences — Meteoric Stones and Shooting Stars—Railway Accidents—Light—Common Things: Air—Locomotion in the United States—Cometary Influences—Common Things: Water—The Potter's Art—Common Things: Fire — Locomotion and Transport, their Influence and Progress—The Moon — Common Things: The Earth — The Electric Telegraph — Terrestrial Heat — The Sun—Earthquakes and Volcanoes—Barometer, Safety Lamp, and Whitworth's Micrometric Apparatus—Steam—The Steam Engine—The Eye — The Atmosphere — Time — Common Things: Pumps—Common Things: Spectacles, the Kaleidoscope — Clocks and Watches — Microscopic Drawing and Engraving—Loco-motive — Thermometer — New Planets: Leverrier and Adams's Planet—Magnitude and Minuteness—Common Things: The Almanack—Optical Images—How to observe the Heavens — Common Things: The Looking-glass — Stellar Universe—The Tides—Colour—Common Things: Man—Magnifying Glasses—Instinct and Intelligence—The Solar Microscope—The Camera Lucida—The Magic Lantern—The Camera Obscura—The Microscope—The White Ants: Their Manners and Habits—The Surface of the Earth, or First Notions of Geography—Science and Poetry—The Bee—Steam Navigation — Electro-Motive Power—Thunder, Lightning, and the Aurora Borealis—The Printing Press—The Crust of the Earth—Comets—The Stereoscope—The Pre-Adamite Earth—Eclipses—Sound.

** OPINIONS OF THE PRESS.

"This series, besides affording popular but sound instruction on scientific subjects, with which the humblest man in the country ought to be acquainted, also undertakes that teaching of 'Common Things' which every well-wisher of his kind is anxious to promote. Many thousand copies of this serviceable publication have been printed, in the belief and hope that the desire for instruction and improvement widely prevails; and we have no fear that such enlightened faith will meet with disappointment."—*Times.*

"A cheap and interesting publication, alike informing and attractive. The papers combine subjects of importance and great scientific knowledge, considerable inductive powers, and a popular style of treatment."—*Spectator.*

"The 'Museum of Science and Art' is the most valuable contribution that has ever been made to the Scientific Instruction of every class of society."—Sir DAVID BREWSTER, in the *North British Review.*

"Whether we consider the liberality and beauty of the Illustrations, the charm of the writing, or the durable interest of the matter, we must express our belief that there is hardly to be found among the new books one that would be welcomed by people of so many ages and classes as a valuable present."—*Examiner.*

** *Separate books formed from the above, suitable for Workmen's Libraries, Science Classes, etc.*

Common Things Explained. Containing Air, Earth, Fire, Water, Time, Man, the Eye, Locomotion, Colour, Clocks and Watches, &c. 233 Illustrations, cloth gilt, 5s.

The Microscope. Containing Optical Images, Magnifying Glasses, Origin and Description of the Microscope, Microscopic Objects, the Solar Microscope, Microscopic Drawing and Engraving, &c. 147 Illustrations, cloth gilt, 2s.

Popular Geology. Containing Earthquakes and Volcanoes, the Crust of the Earth, &c. 201 Illustrations, cloth gilt, 2s. 6d.

Popular Physics. Containing Magnitude and Minuteness, the Atmosphere, Meteoric Stones, Popular Fallacies, Weather Prognostics, the Thermometer, the Barometer, Sound, &c. 85 Illustrations, cloth gilt, 2s. 6d.

Steam and its Uses. Including the Steam Engine, the Locomotive, and Steam Navigation. 89 Illustrations, cloth gilt, 2s.

Popular Astronomy. Containing How to observe the Heavens—The Earth, Sun, Moon, Planets, Light, Comets, Eclipses, Astronomical Influences, &c. 182 Illustrations, 4s. 6d.

The Bee and White Ants: Their Manners and Habits. With Illustrations of Animal Instinct and Intelligence. 135 Illustrations, cloth gilt, 2s.

The Electric Telegraph Popularized. To render intelligible to all who can Read, irrespective of any previous Scientific Acquirements, the various forms of Telegraphy in Actual Operation. 100 Illustrations, cloth gilt, 1s. 6d.

COUNTING-HOUSE WORK, TABLES, etc.

Accounts for Manufacturers.

FACTORY ACCOUNTS: Their Principles and Practice. A Handbook for Accountants and Manufacturers, with Appendices on the Nomenclature of Machine Details; the Income Tax Acts; the Rating of Factories; Fire and Boiler Insurance; the Factory and Workshop Acts, &c., including also a Glossary of Terms and a large number of Specimen Rulings. By EMILE GARCKE and J. M. FELLS. Third Edition. Demy 8vo, 250 pages. price 6s. strongly bound. *[Just published.*

" A very interesting description of the requirements of Factory Accounts. . . . the principle of assimilating the Factory Accounts to the general commercial books is one which we thoroughly agree with."—*Accountants' Journal.*

"Characterised by extreme thoroughness. There are few owners of Factories who would not derive great benefit from the perusal of this most admirable work."—*Local Government Chronicle.*

Foreign Commercial Correspondence.

THE FOREIGN COMMERCIAL CORRESPONDENT: Being Aids to Commercial Correspondence in Five Languages—English, French, German, Italian and Spanish. By CONRAD E. BAKER. Second Edition, Revised. Crown 8vo, 3s. 6d. cloth. *[Just published.*

" Whoever wishes to correspond in all the languages mentioned by Mr. Baker cannot do better than study this work, the materials of which are excellent and conveniently arranged. They consist not of entire specimen letters, but what are far more useful—short passages, sentences, or phrases expressing the same general idea in various forms."—*Athenæum.*

"A careful examination has convinced us that it is unusually complete, well arranged and reliable. The book is a thoroughly good one."—*Schoolmaster.*

Intuitive Calculations.

THE COMPENDIOUS CALCULATOR; or, Easy and Concise Methods of Performing the various Arithmetical Operations required in Commercial and Business Transactions, together with Useful Tables. By DANIEL O'GORMAN. Corrected and Extended by J. R. YOUNG, formerly Professor of Mathematics at Belfast College. Twenty-seventh Edition, carefully Revised by C. NORRIS. Fcap. 8vo, 3s. 6d. strongly half-bound in leather.

" It would be difficult to exaggerate the usefulness of a book like this to everyone engaged in commerce or manufacturing industry. It is crammed full of rules and formulæ for shortening and employing calculations."—*Knowledge.*

"Supplies special and rapid methods for all kinds of calculations. Of great utility to persons engaged in any kind of commercial transactions."—*Scotsman.*

Modern Metrical Units and Systems.

MODERN METROLOGY: A Manual of the Metrical Units and Systems of the Present Century. With an Appendix containing a proposed English System. By LOWIS D'A. JACKSON, A.M.Inst.C.E., Author of " Aid to Survey Practice," &c. Large crown 8vo, 12s. 6d. cloth.

"The author has brought together much valuable and interesting information. . . . We cannot but recommend the work to the consideration of all interested in the practical reform of our weights and measures."—*Nature.*

"For exhaustive tables of equivalent weights and measures of all sorts, and for clear demonstrations of the effects of the various systems that have been proposed or adopted, Mr. Jackson's treatise is without a rival."—*Academy.*

The Metric System and the British Standards.

A SERIES OF METRIC TABLES, in which the British Standard Measures and Weights are compared with those of the Metric System at present in Use on the Continent. By C. H. DOWLING, C.E. 8vo, 10s. 6d. strongly bound.

"Their accuracy has been certified by Professor Airy, the Astronomer-Royal."—*Builder.*

"Mr. Dowling's Tables are well put together as a ready-reckoner for the conversion of one system into the other."—*Athenæum.*

Iron and Metal Trades' Calculator.

THE IRON AND METAL TRADES' COMPANION. For expeditiously ascertaining the Value of any Goods bought or sold by Weight, from 1s. per cwt. to 112s. per cwt., and from one farthing per pound to one shilling per pound. Each Table extends from one pound to 100 tons. To which are appended Rules on Decimals, Square and Cube Root, Mensuration of Superficies and Solids, &c.; Tables of Weights of Materials, and other Useful Memoranda. By THOS. DOWNIE. 396 pp., 9s. Strongly bound in leather.

"A most useful set of tables, and will supply a want, for nothing like them before existed."—*Building News.*

"Although specially adapted to the iron and metal trades, the tables will be found useful in every other business in which merchandise is bought and sold by weight."—*Railway News.*

Calculator for Numbers and Weights Combined.

THE NUMBER AND WEIGHT CALCULATOR. Contain-
ing upwards of 250,000 Separate Calculations, showing at a glance the value
at 421 different rates, ranging from ¼th of a Penny to 20s. each, or per cwt.,
and £20 per ton, of any number of articles consecutively, from 1 to 470.—
Any number of cwts., qrs., and lbs., from 1 cwt. to 470 cwts.—Any number of
tons, cwts., qrs., and lbs., from 1 to 23½ tons. By WILLIAM CHADWICK, Public
Accountant. Second Edition, Revised and Improved, and specially adapted
for the Apportionment of Mileage Charges for Railway Traffic. 8vo, price
18s., strongly bound for Office wear and tear.   [*Just published.*
☞ *This comprehensive and entirely unique and original Calculator is adapted
for the use of Accountants and Auditors, Railway Companies, Canal Companies,
Shippers, Shipping Agents, General Carriers, etc. Ironfounders, Brassfounders,
Metal Merchants, Iron Manufacturers, Ironmongers, Engineers, Machinists, Boiler
Makers, Millwrights, Roofing, Bridge and Girder Makers, Colliery Proprietors, etc.
Timber Merchants, Builders, Contractors, Architects, Surveyors, Auctioneers,
Valuers, Brokers, Mill Owners and Manufacturers, Mill Furnishers, Merchants and
General Wholesale Tradesmen.*

⁎⁎⁎ OPINIONS OF THE PRESS.

The book contains the answers to questions, and not simply a set of ingenious puzzle
methods of arriving at results. It is as easy of reference for any answer or any number of answers
as a dictionary, and the references are even more quickly made. For making up accounts or estimates, the book must prove invaluable to all who have any considerable quantity of calculations
involving price and measure in any combination to do."—*Engineer.*
"The most complete and practical ready reckoner which it has been our fortune yet to see.
It is difficult to imagine a trade or occupation in which it could not be of the greatest use, either
in saving human labour or in checking work. The Publishers have placed within the reach of
every commercial man an invaluable and unfailing assistant."—*The Miller.*
"The most perfect work of the kind yet prepared."—*Glasgow Herald.*

Comprehensive Weight Calculator.

THE WEIGHT CALCULATOR. Being a Series of Tables
upon a New and Comprehensive Plan, exhibiting at One Reference the exact
Value of any Weight from 1 lb. to 15 tons, at 300 Progressive Rates, from 1d.
to 168s. per cwt., and containing 186,000 Direct Answers, which, with their
Combinations, consisting of a single addition (mostly to be performed at
sight), will afford an aggregate of 10,266,000 Answers; the whole being calculated and designed to ensure correctness and promote despatch. By HENRY
HARBEN, Accountant. Fourth Edition, carefully Corrected. Royal 8vo,
strongly half-bound, £1 5s.
"A practical and useful work of reference for men of business generally; it is the best of the
kind we have seen."—*Ironmonger.*
"Of priceless value to business men. It is a necessary book in all mercantile offices."—*Shef-
field Independent.*

Comprehensive Discount Guide.

THE DISCOUNT GUIDE. Comprising several Series of
Tables for the use of Merchants, Manufacturers, Ironmongers, and others,
by which may be ascertained the exact Profit arising from any mode of using
Discounts, either in the Purchase or Sale of Goods, and the method of either
Altering a Rate of Discount or Advancing a Price, so as to produce, by one
operation, a sum that will realise any required profit after allowing one or
more Discounts: to which are added Tables of Profit or Advance from 1¼ to
90 per cent., Tables of Discount from 1½ to 98¾ per cent., and Tables of Com-
mission, &c., from ⅛ to 10 per cent. By HENRY HARBEN, Accountant, Author
of "The Weight Calculator." New Edition, carefully Revised and Corrected.
Demy 8vo, 544 pp. half-bound, £1 5s.
"A book such as this can only be appreciated by business men, to whom the saving of time
means saving of money. We have the high authority of Professor J. R. Young that the tables
throughout the work are constructed upon strictly accurate principles. The work is a model
of typographical clearness, and must prove of great value to merchants, manufacturers, and
general traders."—*British Trade Journal.*

Iron Shipbuilders' and Merchants' Weight Tables.

IRON-PLATE WEIGHT TABLES: For *Iron Shipbuilders,
Engineers and Iron Merchants.* Containing the Calculated Weights of upwards of 150,000 different sizes of Iron Plates, from 1 foot by 6 in. by ¼ in. to
10 feet by 5 feet by 1 in. Worked out on the basis of 40 lbs. to the square
foot of Iron of 1 inch in thickness. Carefully compiled and thoroughly Revised by H. BURLINSON and W. H. SIMPSON. Oblong 4to, 25s. half-bound.
"This work will be found of great utility. The authors have had much practical experience
of what is wanting in making estimates; and the use of the book will save much time in making
elaborate calculations. —*English Mechanic.*

INDUSTRIAL AND USEFUL ARTS.

Soap-making.

THE ART OF SOAP-MAKING : A Practical Handbook of the *Manufacture of Hard and Soft Soaps, Toilet Soaps, etc.* Including many New Processes, and a Chapter on the Recovery of Glycerine from Waste Leys. By ALEXANDER WATT, Author of " Electro-Metallurgy Practically Treated," &c. With numerous Illustrations. Third Edition, Revised. Crown 8vo, 7s. 6d. cloth.

"The work will prove very useful, not merely to the technological student, but to the practical soap-boiler who wishes to understand the theory of his art."—*Chemical News.*
"Really an excellent example of a technical manual, entering, as it does, thoroughly and exhaustively both into the theory and practice of soap manufacture. The book is well and honestly done, and deserves the considerable circulation with which it will doubtless meet."—*Knowledge.*
"Mr. Watt's book is a thoroughly practical treatise on an art which has almost no literature in our language. We congratulate the author on the success of his endeavour to fill a void in English technical literature."—*Nature.*

Paper Making.

THE ART OF PAPER MANUFACTURE : A Practical Hand-*book of the Manufacture of Paper from Rags, Esparto, Wood and other Fibres.* By ALEXANDER WATT, Author of " The Art of Soap-Making," " The Art of Leather Manufacture," &c. With numerous Illustrations. Cr. 8vo. [*In the press.*

Leather Manufacture.

THE ART OF LEATHER MANUFACTURE. Being a Practical Handbook, in which the Operations of Tanning, Currying, and Leather Dressing are fully Described, and the Principles of Tanning Explained, and many Recent Processes introduced; as also Methods for the Estimation of Tannin, and a Description of the Arts of Glue Boiling, Gut Dressing, &c. By ALEXANDER WATT, Author of " Soap-Making," " Electro-Metallurgy," &c. With numerous Illustrations. Second Edition. Crown 8vo, 9s. cloth.

"A sound, comprehensive treatise on tanning and its accessories. . . An eminently valuable production, which redounds to the credit of both author and publishers."—*Chemical Review.*
"This volume is technical without being tedious, comprehensive and complete without being prosy, and it bears on every page the impress of a master hand. We have never come across a better trade treatise, nor one that so thoroughly supplied an absolute want."—*Shoe and Leather Trades' Chronicle.*

Boot and Shoe Making.

THE ART OF BOOT AND SHOE-MAKING. A Practical Handbook, including Measurement, Last-Fitting, Cutting-Out, Closing and Making, with a Description of the most approved Machinery employed. By JOHN B. LENO, late Editor of *St. Crispin,* and *The Boot and Shoe-Maker.* With numerous Illustrations. Third Edition. 12mo, 2s. cloth limp.

"This excellent treatise is by far the best work ever written on the subject. A new work, embracing all modern improvements, was much wanted. This want is now satisfied. The chapter on clicking, which shows how waste may be prevented, will save fifty times the price of the book."—*Scottish Leather Trader.*
"This volume is replete with matter well worthy the perusal of boot and shoe manufacturers and experienced craftsmen, and instructive and valuable in the highest degree to all young beginners and craftsmen in the trade of which it treats."—*Leather Trades' Circular.*

Dentistry.

MECHANICAL DENTISTRY : A Practical Treatise on the *Construction of the various kinds of Artificial Dentures.* Comprising also Useful Formulæ, Tables and Receipts for Gold Plate, Clasps, Solders, &c. &c. By CHARLES HUNTER. Third Edition, Revised. With upwards of 100 Wood Engravings. Crown 8vo, 3s. 6d. cloth.

"The work is very practical."—*Monthly Review of Dental Surgery.*
"We can strongly recommend Mr. Hunter's treatise to all students preparing for the profession of dentistry, as well as to every mechanical dentist."—*Dublin Journal of Medical Science.*
"A work in a concise form that few could read without gaining information from."—*British Journal of Dental Science.*

Wood Engraving.

A PRACTICAL MANUAL OF WOOD ENGRAVING. With a Brief Account of the History of the Art. By WILLIAM NORMAN BROWN. With numerous Illustrations. Crown 8vo, 2s. cloth.

"The author deals with the subject in a thoroughly practical and easy series of representative lessons."—*Paper and Printing Trades Journal.*
"The book is clear and complete, and will be useful to anyone wanting to understand the first elements of the beautiful art of wood engraving."—*Graphic.*

HANDYBOOKS FOR HANDICRAFTS. By PAUL N. HASLUCK.

☞ *These Handybooks are written to supply Handicraftsmen with information on workshop practice, and are intended to convey, in plain language, technical knowledge of the several crafts. Workshop terms are used, and workshop practice described, the text being freely illustrated with drawings of modern tools, appliances and processes.*
N.B. The following Volumes are already published, and others are in preparation

Metal Turning.

THE METAL TURNER'S HANDYBOOK. *A Practical Manual for Workers at the Foot-Lathe:* Embracing Information on the Tools, Appliances and Processes employed in Metal Turning. By PAUL N. HASLUCK, Author of "Lathe-Work." With upwards of One Hundred Illustrations. Second Edition, Revised. **Crown 8vo, 2s. cloth.**

"Altogether admirably adapted to initiate students into the art of turning."—*Leicester Post.*
"Clearly and concisely written, excellent in every way, we heartily commend it to all interested in metal turning."—*Mechanical World.*

Wood Turning.

THE WOOD TURNER'S HANDYBOOK. *A Practical Manual for Workers at the Lathe:* Embracing Information on the Tools, Appliances and Processes Employed in Wood Turning. By PAUL N. HASLUCK. With upwards of One Hundred Illustrations. Crown 8vo, 2s. cloth.

"We recommend the book to young turners and amateurs. A multitude of workmen have hitherto sought in vain for a manual of this special industry."—*Mechanical World.*

Watch Repairing.

THE WATCH JOBBER'S HANDYBOOK. *A Practical Manual on Cleaning, Repairing and Adjusting.* Embracing Information on the Tools, Materials, Appliances and Processes Employed in Watchwork. By PAUL N. HASLUCK. With upwards of One Hundred Illustrations. Cr. 8vo, 2s. cloth.

"All young persons connected with the trade should acquire and study this excellent, and at the same time, inexpensive work."—*Clerkenwell Chronicle.*

Pattern Making.

THE PATTERN MAKER'S HANDYBOOK. A Practical Manual, embracing Information on the Tools, Materials and Appliances employed in Constructing Patterns for Founders. By PAUL N. HASLUCK. With One Hundred Illustrations. Crown 8vo, 2s. cloth.

"We commend it to all who are interested in the counsels it so ably gives."—*Colliery Guardian.*
"This handy volume contains sound information of considerable value to students and artificers."—*Hardware Trades Journal.*

Mechanical Manipulation.

THE MECHANIC'S WORKSHOP HANDYBOOK. *A Practical Manual on Mechanical Manipulation.* Embracing Information on various Handicraft Processes, with Useful Notes and Miscellaneous Memoranda. By PAUL N. HASLUCK. Crown 8vo, 2s. cloth.

"It is a book which should be found in every workshop, as it is one which will be continually referred to for a very great amount of standard information."—*Saturday Review.*

Model Engineering.

THE MODEL ENGINEER'S HANDYBOOK : *A Practical Manual on Model Steam Engines.* Embracing Information on the Tools, Materials and Processes Employed in their Construction. By PAUL N. HASLUCK. With upwards of 100 Illustrations. Crown 8vo, 2s. cloth.

"Mr. Hasluck's latest volume is of greater importance than would at first appear; and indeed he has produced a very good little book."—*Builder.*
"By carefully going through the work, amateurs may pick up an excellent notion of the construction of full-sized steam engines."—*Telegraphic Journal.*

Clock Repairing.

THE CLOCK JOBBER'S HANDYBOOK : *A Practical Manual on Cleaning, Repairing and Adjusting.* Embracing Information on the Tools, Materials, Appliances and Processes Employed in Clockwork. By PAUL N. HASLUCK. With upwards of 100 Illustrations. Cr. 8vo. 2s. cloth. [*Just ready.*

Electrolysis of Gold, Silver, Copper, etc.

ELECTRO-DEPOSITION : A Practical Treatise on the Electrolysis of Gold, Silver, Copper, Nickel, and other Metals and Alloys. With descriptions of Voltaic Batteries, Magneto and Dynamo-Electric Machines, Thermopiles, and of the Materials and Processes used in every Department of the Art, and several Chapters on Electro-Metallurgy. By ALEXANDER WATT, Author of "Electro-Metallurgy," &c. With numerous Illustrations. Third Edition, Revised and Enlarged. Crown 8vo, 9s. cloth.

'Eminently a book for the practical worker in electro-deposition. It contains minute and practical descriptions of methods, processes and materials as actually pursued and used in the workshop. Mr. Watt's book recommends itself to all interested in its subjects."—*Engineer.*

Electro-Metallurgy.

ELECTRO-METALLURGY : Practically Treated. By ALEXANDER WATT, Author of "Electro Deposition," &c. Ninth Edition, including the most recent Processes. 12mo, 4s. cloth boards.

"From this book both amateur and artisan may learn everything necessary for the successful prosecution of electroplating."—*Iron.*

Electroplating.

ELECTROPLATING : A Practical Handbook on the Deposition of Copper, Silver, Nickel, Gold, Aluminium, Brass, Platinum, &c. &c. With Descriptions of the Chemicals, Materials, Batteries and Dynamo Machines used in the Art. By J. W. URQUHART, C.E., Author of "Electric Light," &c. Second Edition, Revised, with Additions. Numerous Illustrations. Crown 8vo, 5s. cloth.

" An excellent practical manual."—*Engineering.*
" This book will show any person how to become an expert in electro-deposition."—*Builder.*
" An excellent work, giving the newest information."—*Horological Journal.*

Electrotyping.

ELECTROTYPING : The Reproduction and Multiplication of Printing Surfaces and Works of Art by the Electro-deposition of Metals. By J. W. URQUHART, C.E. Crown 8vo, 5s. cloth.

" The book is thoroughly practical. The reader is, therefore, conducted through the leading laws of electricity, then through the metals used by electrotypers, the apparatus, and the depositing processes, up to the final preparation of the work."—*Art Journal.*

Goldsmiths' Work.

THE GOLDSMITH'S HANDBOOK. By GEORGE E. GEE, Jeweller, &c. Third Edition, considerably Enlarged. 12mo, 3s. 6d. cloth.

" A good, sound, technical educator, and will be generally accepted as an authority."—*Horological Journal.*
" A standard book which few will care to be without."—*Jeweller and Metalworker.*

Silversmiths' Work.

THE SILVERSMITH'S HANDBOOK. By GEORGE E. GEE, Jeweller, &c. Second Edition, Revised, with Illustrations. 12mo, 3s. 6d. cloth.

" The chief merit of the work is its practical character. . . . The workers in the trade will speedily discover its merits when they sit down to study it."—*English Mechanic.*
** The above two works together, strongly half-bound, price 7s.

Bread and Biscuit Baking.

THE BREAD AND BISCUIT BAKER'S AND SUGAR-BOILER'S ASSISTANT. Including a large variety of Modern Recipes. With Remarks on the Art of Bread-making. By ROBERT WELLS, Practical Baker. Crown 8vo, 2s. cloth. [*Just published.*

" A large number of wrinkles for the ordinary cook, as well as the baker."—*Saturday Review.*
" A book of instruction for learners and for daily reference in the bakehouse."—*Baker's Times.*

Confectionery.

THE PASTRYCOOK AND CONFECTIONER'S GUIDE. For Hotels, Restaurants and the Trade in general, adapted also for Family Use. By ROBERT WELLS, Author of "The Bread and Biscuit Baker's and Sugar Boiler's Assistant." Crown 8vo, 2s. cloth. [*Just published.*

" We cannot speak too highly of this really excellent work. In these days of keen competition our readers cannot do better than purchase this book."—*Baker's Times.*
" Will be found as serviceable by private families as by restaurant *chefs* and victuallers in general."—*Miller.*

Laundry Work.

A HANDBOOK OF LAUNDRY MANAGEMENT. For Use in Steam and Hand-Power Laundries and Private Houses. By the Editor of THE LAUNDRY JOURNAL. Crown 8vo, 2s. 6d. cloth. [*Just published*

Horology.

A TREATISE ON MODERN HOROLOGY, in Theory and Practice. Translated from the French of CLAUDIUS SAUNIER, ex-Director of the School of Horology at Macon, by JULIEN TRIPPLIN, F.R.A.S., Besancon, Watch Manufacturer, and EDWARD RIGG, M.A., Assayer in the Royal Mint. With Seventy-eight Woodcuts and Twenty-two Coloured Copper Plates. Second Edition. Super-royal 8vo, £2 2s. cloth; £2 10s. half-calf.

"There is no horological work in the English language at all to be compared to this production of M. Saunier's for clearness and completeness. It is alike good as a guide for the student and as a reference for the experienced horologist and skilled workman."—Horological Journal.

"The latest, the most complete, and the most reliable of those literary productions to which continental watchmakers are indebted for the mechanical superiority over their English brethren —in fact, the Book of Books, is M. Saunier's 'Treatise.'"—Watchmaker, Jeweller and Silversmith.

Watchmaking.

THE WATCHMAKER'S HANDBOOK. Translated from the French of CLAUDIUS SAUNIER, and considerably Enlarged by JULIEN TRIPPLIN, F.R.A.S., Vice-President of the Horological Institute, and EDWARD RIGG, M.A., Assayer in the Royal Mint. With Numerous Woodcuts and Fourteen Copper Plates. Second Edition. Revised. With Appendix. Cr. 8vo, 9s. cloth.

"Each part is truly a treatise in itself. The arrangement is good and the language is clear and concise. It is an admirable guide for the young watchmaker."—Engineering.

"It is impossible to speak too highly of its excellence. It fulfils every requirement in a handbook intended for the use of a workman. Should be found in every workshop."—Watch and Clockmaker.

CHEMICAL MANUFACTURES & COMMERCE.

Alkali Trade, Manufacture of Sulphuric Acid, etc.

A MANUAL OF THE ALKALI TRADE, including the Manufacture of Sulphuric Acid, Sulphate of Soda, and Bleaching Powder. By JOHN LOMAS, Alkali Manufacturer, Newcastle-upon-Tyne and London. With 232 Illustrations and Working Drawings, and containing 390 pages of Text. Second Edition, with Additions. Super-royal 8vo, £1 10s. cloth.

"This book is written by a manufacturer for manufacturers. The working details of the most approved forms of apparatus are given, and these are accompanied by no less than 232 wood engravings, all of which may be used for the purposes of construction. Every step in the manufacture is very fully described in this manual, and each improvement explained."—Athenæum.

"We find here not merely a sound and luminous explanation of the chemical principles of the trade, but a notice of numerous matters which have a most important bearing on the successful conduct of alkali works, but which are generally overlooked by even experienced technological authors."—Chemical Review.

Brewing.

A HANDBOOK FOR YOUNG BREWERS. By HERBERT EDWARDS WRIGHT, B.A. Crown 8vo, 3s. 6d. cloth.

"This little volume, containing such a large amount of good sense in so small a compass, ought to recommend itself to every brewery pupil, and many who have passed that stage."—Brewers Guardian.

"The book is very clearly written, and the author has successfully brought his scientific knowledge to bear upon the various processes and details of brewing."—Brewer.

Commercial Chemical Analysis.

THE COMMERCIAL HANDBOOK OF CHEMICAL ANALYSIS; or, Practical Instructions for the determination of the Intrinsic or Commercial Value of Substances used in Manufactures, in Trades, and in the Arts. By A. NORMANDY, Editor of Rose's "Treatise on Chemical Analysis." New Edition, to a great extent Re-written by HENRY M. NOAD, Ph.D., F.R.S. With numerous Illustrations. Crown 8vo, 12s. 6d. cloth.

"We strongly recommend this book to our readers as a guide, alike indispensable to the housewife as to the pharmaceutical practitioner."—Medical Times.

"Essential to the analysts appointed under the new Act. The most recent results are given, and the work is well edited and carefully written."—Nature.

Explosives.

A HANDBOOK OF MODERN EXPLOSIVES. Being a Practical Treatise on the Manufacture and Application of Dynamite, Gun-Cotton, Nitro-Glycerine, and other Explosive Compounds. By M. EISSLER, Mining Engineer, Author of "The Metallurgy of Gold," "The Metallurgy of Silver," &c. With about 100 Illustrations. Crown 8vo.   [In the press.

Dye-Wares and Colours.

THE MANUAL OF COLOURS AND DYE-WARES : *Their Properties, Applications, Valuation, Impurities, and Sophistications.* For the use of Dyers, Printers, Drysalters, Brokers, &c. By J. W. SLATER. Second Edition, Revised and greatly Enlarged. Crown 8vo, 7s. 6d. cloth.

"A complete encyclopædia of the *materia tinctoria.* The information given respecting each article is full and precise, and the methods of determining the value of articles such as these, so liable to sophistication, are given with clearness, and are practical as well as valuable."—*Chemist and Druggist.*

"There is no other work which covers precisely the same ground. To students preparing for examinations in dyeing and printing it will prove exceedingly useful."—*Chemical News.*

Pigments.

THE ARTIST'S MANUAL OF PIGMENTS. Showing their Composition, Conditions of Permanency, Non-Permanency, and Adulterations; Effects in Combination with Each Other and with Vehicles ; and the most Reliable Tests of Purity. Together with the Science and Arts Department's Examination Questions on Painting. By H. C. STANDAGE. Second Edition, Revised. Small crown 8vo, 2s. 6d. cloth.

"This work is indeed *multum-in-parvo,* and we can, with good conscience, recommend it to all who come in contact with pigments, whether as makers, dealers or users."—*Chemical Review.*

"This manual cannot fail to be a very valuable aid to all painters who wish their work to endure and be of a sound character ; it is complete and comprehensive."—*Spectator.*

"The author supplies a great deal of very valuable information and memoranda as to the chemical qualities and artistic effect of the principal pigments used by painters."—*Builder.*

Gauging. Tables and Rules for Revenue Officers, Brewers, etc.

A POCKET BOOK OF MENSURATION AND GAUGING : Containing Tables, Rules and Memoranda for Revenue Officers, Brewers, Spirit Merchants, &c. By J. B. MANT (Inland Revenue). Oblong 18mo, 4s. leather, with elastic band.

"This handy and useful book is adapted to the requirements of the Inland Revenue Department, and will be a favourite book of reference. The range of subjects is comprehensive, and the arrangement simple and clear."—*Civilian.*

"A most useful book. It should be in the hands of every practical brewer "—*Brewers' Journal.*

AGRICULTURE, FARMING, GARDENING, etc.

Agricultural Facts and Figures.

NOTE-BOOK OF AGRICULTURAL FACTS AND FIGURES FOR FARMERS AND FARM STUDENTS. By PRIMROSE McCONNELL, Fellow of the Highland and Agricultural Society ; late Professor of Agriculture, Glasgow Veterinary College. Third Edition. Royal 32mo, full roan, gilt edges, with elastic band, 4s.

"The most complete and comprehensive Note-book for Farmers and Farm Students that we have seen. It literally teems with information, and we can cordially recommend it to all connected with agriculture."—*North British Agriculturist.*

Youatt and Burn's Complete Grazier.

THE COMPLETE GRAZIER, and FARMER'S and CATTLE-BREEDER'S ASSISTANT. A Compendium of Husbandry; especially in the departments connected with the Breeding, Rearing, Feeding, and General Management of Stock; the Management of the Dairy, &c. With Directions for the Culture and Management of Grass Land, of Grain and Root Crops, the Arrangement of Farm Offices, the use of Implements and Machines, and on Draining, Irrigation, Warping, &c.; and the Application and Relative Value of Manures. By WILLIAM YOUATT, Esq., V.S. Twelfth Edition, Enlarged by ROBERT SCOTT BURN, Author of "Outlines of Modern Farming," "Systematic Small Farming," &c. One large 8vo volume, 860 pp., with 244 Illustrations, £1 1s. half-bound.

"The standard and text-book with the farmer and grazier."—*Farmer's Magazine.*

"A treatise which will remain a standard work on the subject as long as British agriculture endures."—*Mark Lane Express* (First Notice).

"The book deals with all departments of agriculture, and contains an immense amount of valuable information. It is, in fact, an encyclopædia of agriculture put into readable form, and it is the only work equally comprehensive brought down to present date. It is excellently printed on thick paper, and strongly bound, and deserves a place in the library of every agriculturist."—*Mark Lane Express* (Second Notice).

"This esteemed work is well worthy of a place in the libraries of agriculturists."—*North British Agriculturist.*

Flour Manufacture, Milling, etc.

FLOUR MANUFACTURE: A Treatise on Milling Science
and Practice. By FRIEDRICH KICK, Imperial Regierungsrath, Professor of
Mechanical Technology in the Imperial German Polytechnic Institute,
Prague. Translated from the Second Enlarged and Revised Edition with
Supplement. By H. H. P. POWLES, A.M.I.C.E. Nearly 400 pp. Illustrated
with 28 Folding Plates, and 167 Woodcuts. Royal 8vo, 25s. cloth.

"This valuable work is, and will remain, the standard authority on the science of milling. . . .
The miller who has read and digested this work will have laid the foundation, so to speak, of a successful career; he will have acquired a number of general principles which he can proceed to
apply. In this handsome volume we at last have the accepted text-book of modern milling in good
sound English, which has little, if any, trace of the German idiom."—*The Miller.*
"The appearance of this celebrated work in English is very opportune, and British millers
will, we are sure, not be slow in availing themselves of its pages."—*Millers' Gazette.*

Small Farming.

*SYSTEMATIC SMALL FARMING; or, The Lessons of my
Farm.* Being an Introduction to Modern Farm Practice for Small Farmers.
By ROBERT SCOTT BURN, Author of "Outlines of Modern Farming." With
numerous Illustrations, crown 8vo, 6s. cloth.

"This is the completest book of its class we have seen, and one which every amateur farmer
will read with pleasure and accept as a guide."—*Field.*
"The volume contains a vast amount of useful information. No branch of farming is left
untouched, from the labour to be done to the results achieved. It may be safely recommended to
who think they will be in paradise when they buy or rent a three-acre farm."—*Glasgow Herald.*

Modern Farming.

OUTLINES OF MODERN FARMING. By R. SCOTT BURN.
Soils, Manures, and Crops—Farming and Farming Economy—Cattle, Sheep,
and Horses — Management of Dairy, Pigs and Poultry — Utilisation of
Town-Sewage, Irrigation, &c. Sixth Edition. In One Vol., 1,250 pp., half-
bound, profusely Illustrated, 12s.

"The aim of the author has been to make his work at once comprehensive and trustworthy,
and in this aim he has succeeded to a degree which entitles him to much credit."—*Morning
Advertiser.* "No farmer should be without this book."—*Banbury Guardian.*

Agricultural Engineering.

FARM ENGINEERING, THE COMPLETE TEXT-BOOK OF.
Comprising Draining and Embanking; Irrigation and Water Supply; Farm
Roads, Fences, and Gates; Farm Buildings, their Arrangement and Con-
struction, with Plans and Estimates; Barn Implements and Machines; Field
Implements and Machines; Agricultural Surveying, Levelling, &c. By Prof.
JOHN SCOTT, Professor of Agriculture at the Royal Agricultural College,
Cirencester, &c. In One Vol., 1,150 pages, half-bound, 600 Illustrations, 12s.

"Written with great care, as well as with knowledge and ability. The author has done his
work well; we have found him a very trustworthy guide wherever we have tested his statements.
The volume will be of great value to agricultural students."—*Mark Lane Express.*
"For a young agriculturist we know of no handy volume so likely to be more usefully studied."
—*Bell's Weekly Messenger.*

English Agriculture.

THE FIELDS OF GREAT BRITAIN: A Text-Book of
Agriculture, adapted to the Syllabus of the Science and Art Department.
For Elementary and Advanced Students. By HUGH CLEMENTS (Board of
Trade). Second Edition, Revised and Enlarged. 18mo, 2s. 6d. cloth.

"A most comprehensive volume, giving a mass of information."—*Agricultural Economist.*
"It is a long time since we have seen a book which has pleased us more, or which contains
such a vast and useful fund of knowledge."—*Educational Times.*

New Pocket Book for Farmers.

*TABLES, MEMORANDA, AND CALCULATED RESULTS
for Farmers, Graziers, Agricultural Students, Surveyors, Land Agents Auctioneers, etc.* With a New System of Farm Book-keeping. Selected and
Arranged by SIDNEY FRANCIS. Second Edition, Revised. 272 pp., waistcoat-pocket size, 1s. 6d., limp leather. [*Just published.*

"Weighing less than 1 oz., and occupying no more space than a match box, it contains a mass
of facts and calculations which has never before, in such handy form, been obtainable. Every
operation on the farm is dealt with. The work may be taken as thoroughly accurate, having been
revised by Dr. Fream. We cordially recommend it."—*Bell's Weekly Messenger.*
"A marvellous little book. . . . The agriculturist who possesses himself of it will not be
disappointed with his investment."—*The Farm.*

Farm and Estate Book-keeping.

BOOK-KEEPING FOR FARMERS & ESTATE OWNERS.
A Practical Treatise, presenting, in Three Plans, a System adapted to all Classes of Farms. By JOHNSON M. WOODMAN, Chartered Accountant. Second Edition, Revised. Crown 8vo, 3s. 6d. cloth boards ; or 2s. 6d. cloth limp.
"The volume is a capital study of a most important subject."—*Agricultural Gazette.*
"Will be found of great assistance by those who intend to commence a system of book-keeping, the author's examples being clear and explicit, and his explanations, while full and accurate, being to a large extent free from technicalities."—*Live Stock Journal.*

Farm Account Book.

WOODMAN'S YEARLY FARM ACCOUNT BOOK. Giving a Weekly Labour Account and Diary, and showing the Income and Expenditure under each Department of Crops, Live Stock, Dairy, &c. &c. With Valuation, Profit and Loss Account, and Balance Sheet at the end of the Year, and an Appendix of Forms. Ruled and Headed for Entering a Complete Record of the Farming Operations. By JOHNSON M. WOODMAN, Chartered Accountant, Author of "Book-keeping for Farmers." Folio, 7s. 6d. half bound.   [*culture.*
"Contains every requisite orm for keeping farm accounts readily and accurately."—*Agri-*

Early Fruits, Flowers and Vegetables.

THE FORCING GARDEN ; or, How to Grow Early Fruits, Flowers, and Vegetables. With Plans and Estimates for Building Glasshouses, Pits and Frames. Containing also Original Plans for Double Glazing, a New Method of Growing the Gooseberry under Glass, &c. &c., and on Ventilation, &c. With Illustrations. By SAMUEL WOOD. Crown 8vo, 3s. 6d. cloth.
"A good book, and fairly fills a place that was in some degree vacant. The book is written with great care, and contains a great deal of valuable teaching."—*Gardeners' Magazine.*
"Mr. Wood's book is an original and exhaustive answer to the question 'How to Grow Early Fruits, Flowers and Vegetables?'"—*Land and Water.*

Good Gardening.

A PLAIN GUIDE TO GOOD GARDENING ; or, How to Grow Vegetables, Fruits, and Flowers. With Practical Notes on Soils, Manures, Seeds, Planting, Laying-out of Gardens and Grounds, &c. By S. WOOD. Third Edition, with considerable Additions, &c., and numerous Illustrations. Crown 8vo, 5s. cloth.
"A very good book, and one to be highly recommended as a practical guide. The practical directions are excellent."—*Athenæum.*
"May be recommended to young gardeners, cottagers and amateurs, for the plain and trustworthy information it gives on common matters too often neglected."—*Gardeners' Chronicle.*

Gainful Gardening.

MULTUM-IN-PARVO GARDENING ; or, How to make One Acre of Land produce £620 a-year by the Cultivation of Fruits and Vegetables ; also, How to Grow Flowers in Three Glass Houses, so as to realise £176 per annum clear Profit. By SAMUEL WOOD, Author of "Good Gardening," &c. Fourth and cheaper Edition, Revised, with Additions. Crown 8vo, 1s. sewed.
"We are bound to recommend it as not only suited to the case of the amateur and gentleman's gardener, but to the market grower."—*Gardeners' Magazine.*

Gardening for Ladies.

THE LADIES' MULTUM-IN-PARVO FLOWER GARDEN, and Amateurs' Complete Guide. By S. WOOD. Crown 8vo, 3s. 6d. cloth.
"This volume contains a good deal of sound, common sense instruction."—*Florist.*
"Full of shrewd hints and useful instructions, based on a lifetime of experience."—*Scotsman.*

Receipts for Gardeners.

GARDEN RECEIPTS. Edited by CHARLES W. QUIN. 12mo, 1s. 6d. cloth limp.
"A useful and handy book, containing a good deal of valuable information."—*Athenæum.*

Market Gardening.

MARKET AND KITCHEN GARDENING. By Contributors to "The Garden." Compiled by C. W. SHAW, late Editor of "Gardening Illustrated." 12mo, 3s. 6d. cloth boards.   [*Just published.*
"The most valuable compendium of kitchen and market-garden work published."—*Farmer.*

Cottage Gardening.

COTTAGE GARDENING ; or, Flowers, Fruits, and Vegetables for Small Gardens. By E. HOBDAY. 12mo, 1s. 6d. cloth limp.
"Contains much useful information at a small charge."—*Glasgow Herald.*

ESTATE MANAGEMENT, AUCTIONEERING, LAW, etc.

Hudson's Land Valuer's Pocket-Book.

THE LAND VALUER'S BEST ASSISTANT: Being Tables on a very much Improved Plan, for Calculating the Value of Estates. With Tables for reducing Scotch, Irish, and Provincial Customary Acres to Statute Measure, &c. By R. HUDSON, C.E. New Edition. Royal 32mo, leather, elastic band, 4s.

"This new edition includes tables or ascertaining the value of leases for any term of years; and for showing how to lay out plots of ground of certain acres in forms, square, round, &c., with valuable rules for ascertaining the probable worth of standing timber to any amount; and is of incalculable value to the country gentleman and professional man."—*Farmers' Journal.*

Ewart's Land Improver's Pocket-Book.

THE LAND IMPROVER'S POCKET-BOOK OF FORMULÆ, TABLES and MEMORANDA required in any Computation relating to the Permanent Improvement of Landed Property. By JOHN EWART, Land Surveyor and Agricultural Engineer. Second Edition, Revised. Royal 32mo, oblong, leather, gilt edges, with elastic band, 4s.

"A compendious and handy little volume."—*Spectator.*

Complete Agricultural Surveyor's Pocket-Book.

THE LAND VALUER'S AND LAND IMPROVER'S COMPLETE POCKET-BOOK. Consisting of the above Two Works bound together. Leather, gilt edges, with strap, 7s. 6d.

"Hudson's book is the best ready-reckoner on matters relating to the valuation of land and crops, and its combination with Mr. Ewart's work greatly enhances the value and usefulness of the latter-mentioned. . . . It is most useful as a manual for reference."—*North of England Farmer.*

Auctioneer's Assistant.

THE APPRAISER, AUCTIONEER, BROKER, HOUSE AND ESTATE AGENT AND VALUER'S POCKET ASSISTANT, for the Valuation for Purchase, Sale, or Renewal of Leases, Annuities and Reversions, and of property generally; with Prices for Inventories, &c. By JOHN WHEELER, Valuer, &c. Fifth Edition, re-written and greatly extended by C. NORRIS, Surveyor, Valuer, &c. Royal 32mo, 5s. cloth.

"A neat and concise book of reference, containing an admirable and clearly-arranged list of prices for inventories, and a very practical guide to determine the value of furniture,&c."—*Standard.*

"Contains a large quantity of varied and useful information as to the valuation for purchase, sale, or renewal of leases, annuities and reversions, and of property generally, with prices for inventories, and a guide to determine the value of interior fittings and other effects."—*Builder.*

Auctioneering.

AUCTIONEERS: Their Duties and Liabilities. By ROBERT SQUIBBS, Auctioneer. Demy 8vo, 10s. 6d. cloth.

"The position and duties of auctioneers treated compendiously and clearly."—*Builder.*

"Every auctioneer ought to possess a copy of this excellent work."—*Ironmonger.*

"Of great value to the profession. . . . We readily welcome this book from the fact that it treats the subject in a manner somewhat new to the profession."—*Estates Gazette.*

Legal Guide for Pawnbrokers.

THE PAWNBROKERS', FACTORS' AND MERCHANTS' GUIDE TO THE LAW OF LOANS AND PLEDGES. With the Statutes and a Digest of Cases on Rights and Liabilities, Civil and Criminal, as to Loans and Pledges of Goods, Debentures, Mercantile and other Securities. By H. C. FOLKARD, Esq., Barrister-at-Law, Author of "The Law of Slander and Libel," &c. With Additions and Corrections. Fcap. 8vo, 3s. 6d. cloth.

"This work contains simply everything that requires to be known concerning the department of the law of which it treats. We can safely commend the book as unique and very nearly perfect."—*Iron.*

"The task undertaken by Mr. Folkard has been very satisfactorily performed. . . . Such explanations as are needful have been supplied with great clearness and with due regard to brevity."—*City Press.*

How to Invest.

HINTS FOR INVESTORS : Being an Explanation of the Mode of Transacting Business on the Stock Exchange. To which are added Comments on the Fluctuations and Table of Quarterly Average prices of Consols since 1759. Also a Copy of the London Daily Stock and Share List. By WALTER M. PLAYFORD, Sworn Broker. Crown 8vo, 2s. cloth.

"An invaluable guide to investors and speculators."—*Bullionist*

Metropolitan Rating Appeals.

REPORTS OF APPEALS HEARD BEFORE THE COURT OF GENERAL ASSESSMENT SESSIONS, from the Year 1871 to 1885. By EDWARD RYDE and ARTHUR LYON RYDE. Fourth Edition, brought down to the Present Date, with an Introduction to the Valuation (Metropolis) Act, 1869, and an Appendix by WALTER C. RYDE, of the Inner Temple, Barrister-at-Law. 8vo, 16s. cloth.

" A useful work, occupying a place mid-way between a handbook for a lawyer and a guide to the surveyor. It is compiled by a gentleman eminent in his profession as a land agent, whose specialty, it is acknowledged, lies in the direction of assessing property for rating purposes."—*Land Agents' Record.*

House Property.

HANDBOOK OF HOUSE PROPERTY. *A Popular and Practical Guide to the Purchase, Mortgage, Tenancy, and Compulsory Sale of Houses and Land,* including the Law of Dilapidations and Fixtures; with Examples of all kinds of Valuations, Useful Information on Buildings, and Suggestive Elucidations of Fine Art. By E. L. TARBUCK, Architect and Surveyor. Fourth Edition, Enlarged. 12mo, 5s. cloth.

"The advice is thoroughly practical."—*Law Journal.*
"For all who have dealings with house property, this is an indispensable guide."—*Decoration.*
"Carefully brought up to date, and much improved by the addition of a division on fine art.
 . A well-written and thoughtful work."—*Land Agents' Record*

Inwood's Estate Tables.

TABLES FOR THE PURCHASING OF ESTATES, *Freehold, Copyhold, or Leasehold; Annuities, Advowsons, etc.,* and for the Renewing of Leases held under Cathedral Churches, Colleges, or other Corporate bodies, for Terms of Years certain, and for Lives; also for Valuing Reversionary Estates, Deferred Annuities, Next Presentations, &c.; together with SMART'S Five Tables of Compound Interest, and an Extension of the same to Lower and Intermediate Rates. By W. INWOOD. 23rd Edition, with considerable Additions, and new and valuable Tables of Logarithms for the more Difficult Computations of the Interest of Money, Discount, Annuities, &c., by M. FEDOR THOMAN, of the Société Crédit Mobilier of Paris. Crown 8vo, 8s. cloth.

"Those interested in the purchase and sale of estates, and in the adjustment of compensation cases, as well as in transactions in annuities, life insurances, &c., will find the present edition of eminent service."—*Engineering.*
"'Inwood's Tables' still maintain a most enviable reputation. The new issue has been enriched by large additional contributions by M. Fedor Thoman, whose carefully arranged Tables cannot fail to be of the utmost utility."—*Mining Journal.*

Agricultural and Tenant-Right Valuation.

THE AGRICULTURAL AND TENANT-RIGHT-VALUER'S ASSISTANT. A Practical Handbook on Measuring and Estimating the Contents, Weights and Values of Agricultural Produce and Timber, the Values of Estates and Agricultural Labour, Forms of Tenant-Right-Valuations, Scales of Compensation under the Agricultural Holdings Act, 1883, &c. &c. By TOM BRIGHT, Agricultural Surveyor. Crown 8vo, 3s. 6d. cloth.

"Full of tables and examples in connection with the valuation of tenant-right, estates, labour, contents, and weights of timber, and farm produce of all kinds."—*Agricultural Gazette.*
" An eminently practical handbook, full of practical tables and data of undoubted interest and value to surveyors and auctioneers in preparing valuations ot all kinds."—*Farmer.*

Plantations and Underwoods.

POLE PLANTATIONS AND UNDERWOODS : A Practical Handbook on Estimating the Cost of Forming, Renovating, Improving and Grubbing Plantations and Underwoods, their Valuation for Purposes of Transfer, Rental, Sale or Assessment. By TOM BRIGHT, F.S.Sc., Author of "The Agricultural and Tenant-Right-Valuer's Assistant," &c. Crown 8vo, 3s. 6d. cloth. [*Just published.*

"Very useful to those actually engaged in managing wood."—*Bell's Weekly Messenger.*
" To valuers, foresters and agents it will be a welcome aid."—*North British Agriculturist.*
" Well calculated to assist the valuer in the discharge of his duties, and of undoubted interest and use both to surveyors and auctioneers, in preparing valuations of all kinds."—*Kent Herald.*

A Complete Epitome of the Laws of this Country.

EVERY MAN'S OWN LAWYER: A Handy-Book of the *Principles of Law and Equity.* By A BARRISTER. Twenty-sixth Edition. Reconstructed, Thoroughly Revised, and much Enlarged. Including the Legislation of the Two Sessions of 1888, and including careful digests of *The Local Government Act,* 1888; *County Electors Act,* 1888; *County Courts Act,* 1888; *Glebe Lands Act,* 1888; *Law of Libel Amendment Act,* 1888; *Patents, Designs and Trade Marks Act,* 1888; *Solicitors Act,* 1888; *Preferential Payments in Bankruptcy Act,* 1888; *Land Charges Registration and Searches Act,* 1888; *Trustee Act,* 1888, &c. Crown 8vo, 688 pp., price 6s. 8d. (saved at every consultation!), strongly bound in cloth.   [*Just published.*

** THE BOOK WILL BE FOUND TO COMPRISE (AMONGST OTHER MATTER)—

THE RIGHTS AND WRONGS OF INDIVIDUALS—MERCANTILE AND COMMERCIAL LAW —PARTNERSHIPS, CONTRACTS AND AGREEMENTS—GUARANTEES, PRINCIPALS AND AGENTS—CRIMINAL LAW—PARISH LAW—COUNTY COURT LAW—GAME AND FISHERY LAWS—POOR MEN'S LAWSUITS—LAWS OF BANKRUPTCY—WAGERS—CHEQUES, BILLS AND NOTES—COPYRIGHT—ELECTIONS AND REGISTRATION—INSURANCE—LIBEL AND SLANDER—MARRIAGE AND DIVORCE—MERCHANT SHIPPING—MORTGAGES—SETTLEMENTS—STOCK EXCHANGE PRACTICE—TRADE MARKS AND PATENTS—TRESPASS—NUISANCES—TRANSFER OF LAND—WILLS, &c. &c. Also LAW FOR LANDLORD AND TENANT —MASTER AND SERVANT—HEIRS—DEVISEES AND LEGATEES—HUSBAND AND WIFE— EXECUTORS AND TRUSTEES—GUARDIAN AND WARD—MARRIED WOMEN AND INFANTS —LENDER, BORROWER AND SURETIES—DEBTOR AND CREDITOR—PURCHASER AND VENDOR—COMPANIES—FRIENDLY SOCIETIES—CLERGYMEN—CHURCHWARDENS—MEDICAL PRACTITIONERS—BANKERS—FARMERS—CONTRACTORS—STOCK BROKERS—SPORTSMEN—GAMEKEEPERS—FARRIERS—HORSE DEALERS—AUCTIONEERS—HOUSE AGENTS— INNKEEPERS—BAKERS—MILLERS—PAWNBROKERS—SURVEYORS—RAILWAYS AND CARRIERS—CONSTABLES—SEAMEN—SOLDIERS, &c. &c.

☞ *The following subjects may be mentioned as amongst those which have received special attention during the revision in question:*—Marriage of British Subjects Abroad; Police Constables; Pawnbrokers; Intoxicating Liquors; Licensing; Domestic Servants; Landlord and Tenant; Vendors and Purchasers; Municipal Elections; Local Elections; Corrupt Practices at Elections; Public Health and Nuisances; Highways; Churchwardens; Legal and Illegal Ritual; Vestry Meetings; Rates.

It is believed that the extensions and amplifications of the present edition, while intended to meet the requirements of the ordinary Englishman, will also have the effect of rendering the book useful to the legal practitioner in the country.

One result of the reconstruction and revision, with the extensive additions thereby necessitated, has been *the enlargement of the book by nearly a hundred and fifty pages,* while the price remains as before.

The PUBLISHERS feel every confidence, therefore, that this standard work will continue to be regarded, as hitherto, as an absolute necessity FOR EVERY MAN OF BUSINESS AS WELL AS EVERY HEAD OF A FAMILY.

** OPINIONS OF THE PRESS.

"It is a complete code of English Law, written in plain language, which all can understand. . . . Should be in the hands of every business man, and all who wish to abolish lawyers' bills."— *Weekly Times.*

"A useful and concise epitome of the law, compiled with considerable care. —*Law Magazine.*

"A concise, cheap and complete epitome of the English law. So plainly written that he who runs may read, and he who reads may understand."—*Figaro.*

"A dictionary of legal facts well put together. The book is a very useful one."—*Spectator.*

"A work which has long been wanted, which is thoroughly well done, and which we most cordially recommend."—*Sunday Times.*

Private Bill Legislation and Provisional Orders.

HANDBOOK FOR THE USE OF SOLICITORS AND ENGINEERS Engaged in Promoting Private Acts of Parliament and Provisional Orders, for the Authorization of Railways, Tramways, Works for the Supply of Gas and Water, and other undertakings of a like character. By L. LIVINGSTON MACASSEY, of the Middle Temple, Barrister-at-Law, and Member of the Institution of Civil Engineers; Author of "Hints on Water Supply." Demy 8vo, 950 pp., price 25s. cloth.

"The volume is a desideratum on a subject which can be only acquired by practical experience, and the order of procedure in Private Bill Legislation and Provisional Orders is followed. The author's suggestions and notes will be found of great value to engineers and others professionally engaged in this class of practice."—*Building News.*

"The author's double experience as an engineer and barrister has eminently qualified him for the task, and enabled him to approach the subject alike from an engineering and legal point of view. The volume will be found a great help both to engineers and lawyers engaged in promoting Private Acts of Parliament and Provisional Orders."—*Local Government Chronicle.*

J. OGDEN AND CO. LIMITED, PRINTERS, GREAT SAFFRON HILL, E.C.

www.ingramcontent.com/pod-product-compliance
Lightning Source LLC
Chambersburg PA
CBHW032113010726
47493CB00008B/2560